"Do you have any idea what I thought when I got here and found you gone?"

Daniel's voice was low and barely controlled. "You want to punish me, find a different way."

Rose whirled to face him. He was impossibly close, his stormy eyes blazing with emotions, most of them volatile and dark. "You think I was trying to punish you?"

His expression hardened. "Weren't you?"

"I was following a lead of my own."

"You're a detective now?"

She took a step back and ended up flattened against the door. "You expect me to sit home and play damsel in distress?"

"I expect you to do whatever's necessary to stay alive." He pushed forward, trapping her against the door. "A killer is sending you messages. You fit the profile of his victims."

"I know that."

He caught her shoulders in his hands, his fingers strong and sharp against her shirt. "Then act like it."

And before she could respond, his lips covered hers....

PAULA GRAVES

FORBIDDEN TEMPTATION

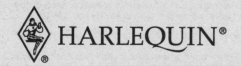

TORONTO • NEW YORK • LONDON
AMSTERDAM • PARIS • SYDNEY • HAMBURG
STOCKHOLM • ATHENS • TOKYO • MILAN • MADRID
PRAGUE • WARSAW • BUDAPEST • AUCKLAND

For my girls —
Melissa, Ashlee, Sarah, Amber and Kathryn.

ISBN-13: 978-0-373-69265-1
ISBN-10:   0-373-69265-X

FORBIDDEN TEMPTATION

Copyright © 2007 by Paula Graves

www.eHarlequin.com

Printed in U.S.A.

ABOUT THE AUTHOR

Alabama native Paula Graves wrote her first book, a mystery starring herself and her neighborhood friends, at the age of six. A voracious reader, Paula loves books that pair tantalizing mystery with compelling romance. When she's not reading or writing, she works as a creative director for a Birmingham advertising agency and spends time with her family and friends. She is a member of Southern Magic Romance Writers, Heart of Dixie Romance Writers and Romance Writers of America.

Paula invites readers to visit her Web site, www.paulagraves.com.

Books by Paula Graves

HARLEQUIN INTRIGUE
926—FORBIDDEN TERRITORY
998—FORBIDDEN TEMPTATION

CAST OF CHARACTERS

Rose Browning—The wedding planner sees "death veils" on the faces of people destined to die at the hands of a brutal serial killer. Does she have a psychic connection to the killer?

Daniel Hartman—The former FBI profiler believes the murders are the work of Orion, a prolific serial killer Daniel has tracked across eight states. Did Orion kill Daniel's fiancée, Tina, thirteen years ago?

Frank Carter—Tina's younger brother joined the police force after his sister's death. Can he help Daniel find her killer?

Melissa Bannerman—Though she tries to heed Rose's warnings, the unlucky bride-to-be never makes it to the altar.

Jesse Phillips—The security system technician worked for two of the killer's victims. Could he be connected to the murders in a more sinister way?

Mark Phagan—Melissa's fiancé has a dark side. Did he stage his bride-to-be's death to look like the work of the serial killer?

Captain Green—The police captain isn't happy to find herself saddled with a serial killer, a freelance profiler and a witness who sees visions of death.

Iris Browning and Lily McBride—Rose's sisters don't understand Rose's sudden change of personality.

J. McBride—Rose's brother-in-law wonders why a former hot shot FBI profiler is asking questions about his sister-in-law.

Prologue

A brisk December wind moaned in the pines, driving Rose Browning deeper into her long wool coat. She adjusted the basket of muffins hanging at a dangerous tilt in the crook of her left arm, breathing in the warm aroma of cinnamon that almost overpowered the tang of pine needles and fallen leaves carpeting the path through Bridey Woods.

The ramshackle facade of Carrie and Dillon Granville's home came into view. Her pulse quickening, Rose crunched over the frosty ground, speeding up the closer she got. In a minute, Carrie would open the door and smile her welcome, her expression blurred by a shimmer of transparent silver in the shape of her husband Dillon's face. Dillon would appear in the door behind his wife, his smile harder to come by, but that wouldn't matter once Rose saw the image of Carrie dancing over his face.

This was the best part of what she did, getting to see the veils, each time like the first, fresh and wonderful.

She called them true-love veils, shimmery images of soul mates superimposed over each other's faces. Seeing them was her gift, and she'd helped a lot of soul mates find each other over the years. She'd even made a career out of it, planning weddings for the people she brought together.

It was how she'd known that Carrie and Dillon were meant to be together, despite the obstacles keeping them apart.

The true-love veils were the best gift in the world, and she was grateful to be the Browning sister who'd received it.

Rose's footsteps rang on the rickety porch steps, usually enough to bring the sound of feet moving across the rough wood floor inside. But this morning she heard only a low keening sound, which seemed to echo the December wind in the towering pines overhead, sending a chill curling down her spine.

She lifted her hand to knock but faltered, unease slithering through her belly. The woods around her lay silent, as if the animals were in hiding. She'd heard the bark of a gun as she'd left her house near town but thought little of it. Hunting season was in full swing, and, while Willow Grove, Alabama, could boast of lush green fields to lure hunters from the city, many of the locals couldn't afford to be so picky.

Maybe a hunter had spooked the animals, she told herself.

But she didn't quite believe it.

The keening grew louder. Harsh breathing, she realized, her nerves jangling. Coming from inside.

"Carrie?"

The breathing stopped.

Rose took a reluctant step closer to the cracked-open door. She could see nothing through the dark opening.

"Carrie? It's Rose. Is everything okay?"

The silence stretched and grew taut. Rose leaned toward the narrow opening, trying to peer into the darkness.

Overhead a crow shrieked; the raucous sound was like a knife sawing over her tight nerves. Rose jerked, her hand smacking into the door, stinging her cold knuckles. She swallowed a hiss of pain as the door creaked open, hinges moaning.

Daylight slashed across the dark interior to reveal Carrie Granville's arm outstretched across the plank floor of the main room. The rest of her body was hidden in shadow.

As Rose's heart clenched, something dark, thick and fluid slithered across the floor toward Carrie's hand.

Blood.

Rose took a step back, until a soft snicking sound brought her to a dead halt.

"She made me do it." Dillon Granville's country twang emerged from the shadows, low and pained. "I didn't want to, but she made me."

Wind gusted at Rose's back, blowing her dark hair into her eyes and pushing the door into the wall. Daylight flooded the cabin's interior.

Dillon squinted at the sudden light, giving Rose time to turn and run. But what she saw on his face froze her in place.

The true-love veil was there, just as she'd imagined it: Carrie's face, smiling and happy, a horrific contrast to the slack, pallid face of the woman lying dead on the floor, her eyes half open and forever sightless.

Rose's arms fell weakly to her sides. Her Christmas

basket hit the porch with a thud, spilling apple-cinnamon muffins across the weathered planks.

Behind the lingering true-love veil, Dillon's expression shifted, hardened. Rose's heart jolted.

"I can't live without her. It's like you told us. We're supposed to be together forever." As the hardness of Dillon's expression softened into a distant half smile, the veil over his face rippled, slowly changing to a translucent image of his own face, his left temple open and pulpy.

Before Rose could process what she was seeing, Dillon lifted the gun. Ice gushed into Rose's veins and she took a stumbling step back, her legs heavy and unresponsive.

The gun barrel was pointed in her direction for only the briefest moment on its way up to Dillon's right temple.

"No." Rose's voice came out strangled, watery with horror.

Dillon smiled at her. "Together forever," he said.

Then he pulled the trigger.

Chapter One

The woman sat alone at a table near the narrow stage at the front of the bar, nursing a strawberry daiquiri and feigning interest in the alt-rock cover band currently grinding its way through an old Pearl Jam classic. Now and then she took a sip of her drink but mainly watched the crowd, her eyes alert.

Daniel Hartman studied her from his seat at the bar, curiosity distracting him from his own agenda. There was an odd stillness about her, a composure that set her apart from the rest of the restless liquor-soaked crowd in the small club in the heart of Birmingham's Five Points South.

Who was she? What was she looking for?

The door opened and a man in a striped shirt and leather jacket entered, pausing in the doorway. Daniel dragged his attention away from the woman to give the newcomer a quick once-over. He was pushing forty, a little paunchy though his clothes hid it well. The wedding ring on his left hand quickly went into his pocket.

Classy.

Daniel looked away, losing interest. This place was

a bust. He took another sip of Coke and considered moving on to another club a few doors down. But his gaze drifted back to the woman with the daiquiri, and he stayed put, watching her through narrowed eyes as she took another dainty sip of her drink and clapped politely as the cover band crashed its way to the end of the song.

The paunchy man in the leather jacket approached her table, on the prowl. Of course he'd choose her—a pretty woman all alone in the middle of a bar was too much temptation. Daniel sat forward, curious to see how she'd handle being hit on. Would she notice the imprint on his left ring finger where the wedding band had been? Would it matter?

She looked up at the man, her brow furrowing as he spoke to her. Her gaze drifted to the hand resting on the back of her chair and the furrowed brow smoothed, replaced by a cool, neutral mask. She murmured to the man, who stepped away with a frown. Muttering something that made the woman's lips tighten, he moved on to the bar and ordered a bourbon neat.

Daniel looked back at the woman and found her watching him. When she didn't immediately look away, he lifted his glass and nodded.

Her frown returning, she looked down at her glass, stirring the red slush with slow, deliberate strokes. Her chin lifted, followed by her eyes. She locked gazes with him, her expression impossible to read. An electric shock zigzagged through him as he took the full brunt of her attention.

Was it an invitation? A rebuff? He didn't know, and he'd always prided himself on being an accomplished reader of women. Of people, in general, given his chosen profession.

He could look around this bar and guess, with accuracy, the stories behind the faces surrounding him: The balding salesman with the desperate come-on sitting with the aging beauty queen who'd accepted his offer of a drink because she was desperate for the attention she used to command without effort. The raw-nerved coed drinking to forget her cheating boyfriend and her unfinished term paper. The tax accountant sipping a trendy dark ale and trying to look as though he was just one of the guys. Daniel could read them all.

But not her.

She looked across the room and caught the eye of a waitress, who came at once. They murmured an exchange and the waitress went toward the back, soon returning with the check.

The woman paid her bill and rose from the table, darting a glance in his direction. He followed her with his gaze, memorizing the curve of her hips and the dip of her narrow waist, the way her calf muscles flexed as she navigated the crowded club and pushed her way through the exit door into the cool October night. His skin felt hot and tight.

Part of him wanted desperately to follow her, to see where she went next. What was she looking for? Would she find it?

But he had a job to do here, a job that didn't include tailing pretty brunettes with great legs. He stayed where he was, waving at the bartender to pour him another Coke. The bartender complied, giving him a black look because he wasn't buying pricey liquor to go with the soda. Daniel couldn't blame him—the bar didn't make money off designated drivers.

But he needed his wits about him tonight.

ROSE LOCKED THE CAR DOOR behind her and closed her eyes, giving in to the tremor in her legs.

Was he the one?

She thought she'd know it immediately, that the rage and violence roiling inside him would surely show on his face, but the man at the bar had looked so normal. Attractive, even, with masculine features, eyes the gray of a winter sky and a lean swimmer's build. The kind of man she might have smiled at a year ago, encouraged to join her in a drink and some friendly conversation.

But she wasn't that woman anymore.

She put the key in the ignition and turned it. The engine purred to life, the heater vents blowing cool air in a blast that amplified her shivers.

She tightened her sweater around her and turned on the CD player. Allison Krauss's clarion voice flowed from the speakers, a plaintive plea to a potential lover to let her touch him for a while. She punched the power button off with a growl, glancing at her rearview mirror, where the front entrance of the Southside Pub reflected back at her in garish neon. Part of her expected the door to open and the man from the bar to emerge, seeking her out.

Stalking her.

Another part of her was disappointed when he didn't.

She glanced at the dashboard clock. Only nine-fifteen on a Friday. The night was young. There were at least half a dozen more bars just in the Five Points South area she could visit before closing time.

Her chest tightened at the thought, but she tamped down her reluctance and pulled her Chevy into the moderate traffic on Twentieth Street, heading for the next bar on her list.

She found one of the last parking places on a side street where two bars sat side by side, as different from each other as day and night. Hannity's, an old-fashioned Irish pub complete with green neon shamrocks in the window, occupied the corner. Next door was Sizzle, unmistakably a dance bar with flashing lights and a driving bass beat she could hear from her car.

She headed for the dance bar, steeling herself for the noise and light. Southside Pub had been sedate in comparison. Sizzle's clientele was a good decade younger and twice as loud. At twenty-seven, she was one of the oldest women in the place. Her skirt was at least five inches too long, her silk blouse not nearly tight enough and her upswept hair prim compared to the flying tresses of the women gyrating on the dance floor.

She quelled the urge to head right back out the door, reminding herself that Elisa Biondi had last been seen at this very bar the night she died.

He came to places like this. He looked for women on their own. Easy targets.

She felt an invisible bull's-eye sitting between her shoulder blades as she weaved through the restless crowd and found a seat at the bar.

"Virgin daiquiri," she ordered, ignoring the bartender's arched brow. Had the woman never heard of designated drivers?

The bartender mixed the drink, leaving out the rum, and slid it down the bar to Rose. "Knock yourself out."

Ignoring the mild gibe, Rose paid for the drink and sipped the sweet slush through her straw, turning her gaze toward the club floor. Dancers filled the cramped space, most of them moving with more enthusiasm than skill, their focus on seduction rather than rhythm. Faces blended into one another, merging into an undulating mass of color and motion.

"Rose?"

The sound of her name drew Rose's attention away from the dance floor. She turned to find Melissa Bannerman, her current client, sitting at a table nearby, sipping a margarita. Melissa motioned her over.

Picking up her daiquiri, Rose crossed to the table, relieved to see a familiar face. "No Mark?" she asked Melissa, referring to her client's fiancé.

Melissa hesitated before responding. "He's in Knoxville for the Bama-Tennessee game. I have a stack of unread manuscripts to get through this weekend, so I couldn't get away." Melissa's family owned a small publishing company. "Have a seat. I promise we won't talk wedding business."

Rose took one of the empty seats. Melissa was obviously not alone; someone's drink sat on the table in front of one of the other chairs. "I shouldn't barge in on your night out—"

"Alice won't mind." Melissa waved toward the dance floor. "We'll be lucky if we see her the rest of the night. She just broke up with her scummy boyfriend and I think she plans to dance with every guy in this place. Therapy, you know?" A hint of bitterness tinged Melissa's words. She'd almost ended her engagement a year earlier after catching Mark cheating. Mark's promise never to stray again had kept the engagement intact. Rose wasn't sure Melissa had made the right decision.

The true-love veils had made it so much easier to know if a couple was about to make a big mistake.

"Look at her go," Melissa said with a chuckle.

Rose followed Melissa's gaze and spotted a tall, curvy woman with wavy brown hair. Her back was to Rose and Melissa, her body grooving to the pounding bass coming from the giant speakers on the wall. Her dance partner could barely keep up, but he didn't look unhappy about it, his eyes wide with male appreciation as his partner danced off her frustrations.

Alice turned her back on him, a not-so-subtle reminder that she was here for the music, not the man. She looked at the table where Rose and Melissa sat, waggling her fingers at them.

Rose sucked in a swift breath.

Alice's face was covered with a shimmery silver veil.

Rose called them death veils for lack of a better term. She'd seen several since Dillon Granville's suicide, death masks superimposed over the faces of the doomed, a gruesome contrast to the true-love veils she'd seen all her life up to that horrible day in Bridey Woods.

The particular death veil Alice wore was one Rose had seen before, six weeks ago on the face of a woman at the grocery store where Rose shopped. Three days later, she'd been found murdered near the Birmingham

Zoo. Two weeks ago, Rose had seen the same kind of veil on the face of a cyclist riding in front of her house. She'd been found murdered, as well.

News reports hadn't mentioned their wounds, but Rose knew what they'd been. Slashes across their jawlines and foreheads. Gouges on the soft apples of their cheeks. And a ragged slit across each of their throats, the killing blow.

Two women dead, and Rose had foreseen their murders. How many others hadn't she seen?

She stared at Alice, transfixed by the shimmer of death on her pretty face. What now? Tell Melissa what she was seeing? She discarded the idea immediately. Melissa might be unpredictable and impulsive, but beneath it all was a solid strain of rationality, and what Rose could see was about as irrational as it got.

Would Alice be more open? How long did Rose have to convince her? Would the killer strike tomorrow?

Tonight?

A finger of dread traced an icy path up Rose's spine. Was he here already? Hidden by the throngs, watching Alice dance and imagining what he was going to do to her?

Fear rose in her throat, nearly gagging her.

The song ended and Alice crossed to their table. She dropped into the chair in front of the half-empty beer bottle. "Whew! That was fun."

"Richard who?" Melissa teased.

Alice laughed, her eyes crinkling with good humor. "Exactly." She turned to Rose. "Hi. I'm Alice."

"I'm Rose."

"Sorry—how rude of me!" Melissa gestured to

Alice. "This is Alice Donovan, the dancing queen. We went to college together at Bama. Alice, this is Rose Browning, my wedding planner. I told you about her."

Alice grinned at Rose, the expression grotesquely juxtaposed against the blood-streaked death veil hovering over her face. Rose swallowed the bile rising in her throat and managed a smile in return.

"You should give Rose your card, Alice. Alice just opened a florist shop down the street from here," Melissa explained.

"Really? I'll be sure to give you a call," Rose said, tamping down her growing distress.

"Great!" Alice pulled a card out of her clutch purse and handed it to Rose. "We're brand-new, but we have terrific suppliers, and I think you'll be very pleased with our work."

Rose tucked the card into her purse and took a deep breath, wondering what to say next. A lot of people claimed interest in the paranormal, but even if Alice wasn't a stone-cold skeptic, would she really believe that Rose could foresee her death? What person would want to hear something like that, much less put any stock in it?

True-love veils had been easier to talk about. Everybody wanted to believe in happily-ever-after.

"Listen, I hate to boogie and run, but the shop opens tomorrow bright and early." Alice slid her chair back and took a last swallow of beer on the table in front of her. She turned to Rose. "It was nice meeting you. Give me a call and we can discuss what I can do for your business."

Now, Rose thought. *Tell her now. Just blurt it out.*

"I'll do that," she said, kicking herself for her cowardice. "First thing in the morning."

Alice flashed her another smile beneath the death veil and headed for the exit.

Rose watched her go, wondering if he would follow her out. Could it be that simple? Was he here in the crowd, waiting for his chance? Waiting fifteen seconds or twenty, enough that nobody would notice him following her, but not so long that he couldn't catch up with her before she reached her car?

Rose counted the seconds in her mind. Five. Ten. Fifteen…

Nobody followed Alice out of the bar.

Rose clutched her purse and turned to Melissa. "I've got to run, too, Melissa—I almost forgot about a meeting I have first thing in the morning." She rose from the table.

"The new caterer?"

"Yes," Rose lied, already on her way to the exit, heading off any more questions from Melissa.

Outside, she scanned the street for a glimpse of Alice Donovan. There weren't many parking places near the bar. Rose had lucked into her spot a few cars down. There had to be a parking lot somewhere nearby—

She spotted a sign that said Free Parking and followed the arrow to a side lot around the corner of the Irish pub. There. She spotted Alice opening the door of a dark blue Camry.

Quelling her fear, she called out Alice's name, jogging toward her across the narrow lot.

Alice turned at the sound, her brow crinkling until

she recognized Rose. "Oh, hi. Did I leave something in the bar?"

Rose faltered to a stop, taking a deep breath to brace herself. "I have to tell you something, and you're going to think it sounds crazy, but I need you to hear me out."

Alice's eyes narrowed. "What are you talking about?"

Rose licked her lips. "I see things. I guess, you might call them visions—sort of. Not exactly." She grimaced as Alice's expression darkened. "Do you remember the U.A.B. student who was murdered a couple of weeks ago?"

Alice's expression shifted from wary to alarmed. "Yes."

"The day before she died, I saw her riding her bike in front of my house. Over her face was this…thing. I call it a veil—it's like a shimmery image superimposed over her face. Her own face, only…dead."

Alice took a step back, her fingers closing around her car keys. "Look, I've got to go—"

Rose took a desperate step forward. "I know it sounds crazy. I know it does. But I saw the death veil and then she died. I saw another woman a few weeks ago—the same thing. Her face, slashed and bloody. She turned up dead three days later."

Alice shook her head. "Why are you telling me this?"

"Because I see a death veil on you," Rose blurted.

Alice's eyes narrowed to slits. "You're right. You sound crazy." She unlocked her car door, keeping her eyes on Rose. "We'll chalk this up to too much rum, okay? I'm leaving now."

"Just be careful, Alice. I don't care if you think I'm crazy, as long as you remember what I told you."

Alice opened the car door, turning her back on Rose only at the last moment, when she slid behind the wheel and slammed the door shut behind her. Rose heard the click of the automatic locks engaging and released a pent-up breath.

The Camry's engine fired to life, forcing Rose to step out of the way to let Alice pull out of the parking space. The Camry wheeled around and headed out of the small lot, pulling into the light traffic headed toward Twentieth Street.

Rose's knees began to shake. She leaned against the car parked next to the now-empty slot. Closing her eyes, she gave in to the tremors rolling through her.

Okay. It hadn't been pleasant, but she'd warned Alice of the danger. Maybe it would be enough. Maybe she'd do something different, be a little more alert over the next couple of days. Avoid being alone where someone could take advantage of her vulnerability.

Alone.

As she was now, in the middle of this isolated parking lot, with only the muddy yellow streetlamp on the corner to chase away the evening gloom. Dread slithered through her belly.

She was alone.

Vulnerable.

The hairs on her neck rose. She felt eyes on her, as tangible as the mist of her breath in the cold night air.

She whirled around and peered into the darkness at the far end of the parking lot. She saw only blackness, impenetrable and infinite. But somewhere in that abyss, someone was watching. Waiting.

Swallowing her rising panic, Rose turned and ran,

her heels clattering on the uneven blacktop. She reached the sidewalk and looked behind her at the far end of the parking lot.

Something moved, darting through the gloom and disappearing behind the pub.

Her pulse hammering in her ears, Rose raced to her car, oblivious to the stares of the scattered pedestrians dotting the sidewalk. She fumbled with her keys, her breath coming in soft, keening gasps, until she managed to unlock the Impala's door. She slid inside, pulling the door shut so quickly that she almost caught her foot.

She jabbed at the power lock. The levers snicked softly as they slid into place, closing her safely inside.

In the silence, her breathing was harsh and rapid. She forced herself to let her heart rate settle into a less frantic cadence before she put the key in the ignition.

She hadn't been imagining it, had she? She'd seen movement in the shadows, felt his gaze like a touch. She wasn't crazy.

He'd been watching Alice. Waiting for his opportunity. Maybe he would have made his move right there in the parking lot, if Rose hadn't showed up.

Maybe she'd already saved Alice Donovan's life.

But now the killer had seen her.

Rose grabbed the rearview mirror, positioning it to see her own reflection. Her eyes, dark with fear, stared back at her, but her face was clear. No death veil.

She slumped against the car seat, relief tingling through her, quickly swamped by guilt. So what if she was safe? Alice Donovan was still in danger, and Rose's clumsy attempt to warn her had failed. If her warning had changed Alice's fate, wouldn't the death veil have disappeared?

She lowered her forehead to the steering wheel, feeling sick. The truth was, she didn't know if the death veil would have disappeared. She knew nothing about the damned things, except that they had made her life a constant misery for the past ten months.

She gave herself a shake. Maybe she was giving up too soon. The other victims hadn't died immediately. A day or two had passed before their bodies were found. Alice had said she was going straight home; maybe the killer wouldn't strike tonight.

She still had Alice's business card and the phone number to her florist shop. She could call Alice in the morning, apologize for scaring her and try to explain things more coherently.

Maybe it would work.

She forced her rubbery limbs into motion, buckling her seat belt and starting the car. The dashboard clock showed ten twenty-five. The night was still young, by Friday-night-clubbing standards, but she'd seen all the death veils she could bear in one evening.

She pulled carefully into traffic and circled the block, coming to stop at the traffic light in front of the Storyteller fountain. Spotlights in the center of the fountain lit up the whimsical bronze sculpture of a ram dressed as a man reading to an assembly of smaller bronze animals. A young couple sat on a bench nearby, holding hands and gazing at each other, oblivious to the beauty of the fountain.

A few months ago Rose could have known at a glance whether or not the couple was destined to love each other for a lifetime. Now all she could say, for sure, was that neither of them was destined to die in the next few days.

She looked up at the red light, willing it to change.

A cluster of pedestrians crossed in front of her, heading toward the fountain. A dark-haired man brought up the rear, his long trench coat flapping with each confident stride. A flutter of awareness sparked in Rose's belly as she recognized him.

The stranger who'd been watching her at the Southside Pub.

He turned his face toward her as if he could sense her scrutiny. Rose shrank back into the shadows, knowing that the glare of the streetlamp off her windshield most likely hid her from his view. The light changed to green as he reached the sidewalk by the fountain, but Rose didn't move. Adrenaline rushed into her bloodstream.

He'd come from the direction of the club she'd just left.

Behind her, a horn honked, rattling her nerves. She accelerated across the intersection, her heart rate picking up speed. She took a left at the next intersection, heading toward Mountain Avenue. Just a few blocks and she'd be home. Safe.

At least, for now.

MIDNIGHT HAD COME and gone, but Rose remained curled up in the overstuffed armchair by the front windows, gazing out at the moonless night. The lights of the city cast a yellow haze across the night sky, obscuring the stars from her view.

She closed her eyes and listened to the thud of her

pulse in her ears, steady and just a little rapid, still pumped up with adrenaline from the evening's events. Behind her eyelids, the sight of Alice Donovan's scarred and bleeding face played in strobing slow motion, like a silent movie.

A scratching sound at the front door jerked her eyes open. Staring at the solid door, she held her breath, wondering if she'd imagined it.

Then she heard it again. It was faint but unmistakable, a discordant sound, as if someone were scraping fingernails down the outside of the door.

Releasing a shaky breath, Rose crept to the door and peered through the fish-eye lens. She could see nothing outside.

Checking to make sure the safety chain was engaged, she unlocked the dead bolt and cracked the door open.

Alice Donovan's wide, sightless green eyes stared up at Rose from the welcome mat. Blood from the gashes in her face flowed onto the concrete stoop, the crimson turned black in the muddy yellow light from the street-lamps.

Alice's lips moved slowly, a soft rattle rising from her ruined throat. "Too…late—"

Rose jerked awake, her heart in her throat. It was still nighttime, the clock over the mantel reading 2:00 a.m. She sat in the armchair by the window, her back and legs aching from the cramped position.

Her pulse thundered in her ears, beating out a guilty cadence.

Too late.

Too late.

Too late.

Chapter Two

Rose called the flower shop as early as she dared the next morning. As soon as someone answered the phone, she forced the reluctant words from her mouth. "Is Alice Donovan there?"

"She's not in yet."

"When do you expect her in?"

A thick pause greeted the question. When the woman finally spoke, the anxiety in her voice was palpable. "An hour ago."

Rose's nightmare flashed through her mind, chilling her to the bone. Her voice cracked. "Have you tried her home number?"

"She's not answering her home phone or her cell." The woman's voice shook. "She's never late like this."

Rose tried to keep her voice even. "I met her last night. I said I'd give her a call—I'm a wedding planner and I can always use a new flower source."

"Was she okay when you saw her?"

Rose closed her eyes. "She was fine, heading home the last I talked to her. Does she live nearby?"

"On Doberville—the Brookstone Apartments."

Rose gave a start. A block away, easy walking distance.

"I'd go check on her," the woman continued, "but I'm the only one in the shop…."

"I'll check, if you'd like. I live nearby. What apartment?"

The woman hesitated, as if realizing she'd already given out a lot of personal information to a stranger. "Maybe I should call the police."

"Definitely do that. But they won't do anything yet— she's an adult and she's been missing only an hour. I know you don't want to give out that kind of information to a stranger on the phone. My name is Rose Browning. Like I said, I have a wedding planning company. You can look me up in the Yellow Pages or on the Internet. I just want to help, and I live so close…"

"Apartment 2-D," the woman said softly.

"I'll go right now." Rose hung up and started dressing, trying to convince herself that she wasn't too late.

That Alice wasn't already dead.

THE MORNING CHILL curled around the collar of Daniel's suit jacket, making him wish he'd worn an overcoat. Ahead, yellow crime tape cordoned off a large square where the crime-scene unit gathered evidence while detectives watched from the sides.

Daniel steered clear of the tape, blending into the crowd of locals watching from across the street. He edged toward the local television reporters setting up for live shots nearby.

A pretty black woman in a red wool coat was doing sound checks, practicing her copy for the technician.

"Police report that a couple of joggers found the body here just outside the Mountain View Golf Course. Police have not identified the victim, a woman in her mid-twenties."

An image of the dark-haired woman at the Southside Pub flashed through Daniel's mind. Unease settled low in his gut.

He needed to see the body. See who she was, if she was displayed. The crime-scene unit surrounded the body, their camera flashes piercing the tree-sheltered gloom of the brush bordering the golf course.

He circled the scene, vines and brambles tugging his pant cuffs as he edged away from the sightseers and climbed a slight rise for a better vantage point. He settled between a couple of trees. His line of sight wasn't perfect, but he had a pretty good view of the body. He pulled a small pair of binoculars from his jacket pocket and trained them on the scene.

Though nobody looked the same in death as in life, he quickly ascertained that the woman lying faceup in the tall grass was not the dark-haired beauty he'd seen at the pub the night before. This woman was about the same age, but her hair was lighter in color, with an unruly wave to it.

Ignoring a twinge of relief, he trained the binoculars on the victim's face. He could see little of her features behind the roadmap of slashes marring her pale skin, but what he saw of the wound patterns answered the most pressing question. She was victim number three. She lay posed on her back with her hands crossed over her chest, just like the others.

Just like Tina.

"Danny?"

A man's voice nearby sent a jolt down Daniel's spine. He turned to find a clean-cut man in a trim gray suit standing a few feet away, his head slightly cocked.

Daniel was mentally prepping his explanation when he realized the man had called him by name. Recognition dawned, unexpected and not entirely welcome.

No longer the gangly teen Daniel had known, Tina Carter's brother, Frank, was now in his thirties. He'd gone from bony to wellbuilt and, while still not exactly handsome, women would like him, especially with the badge hanging low on his hip.

Daniel pocketed his binoculars. "Didn't know you'd become a detective, Frank." He crossed to the man and held out his hand.

Frank shook it firmly. "You didn't know I was on the force at all, Danny." He shrugged off Daniel's apologetic expression. "What are you doing here? Nobody called the FBI."

"I'm not with the FBI anymore. I teach college now." Daniel nodded toward the crime scene. "This is number three, isn't it? Here, at least."

Frank glanced toward the scene. "Why would a college professor want to know?"

"Just looking."

Frank's frown tightened. "I've got to get back before my captain realizes I'm not around. I suggest you be gone before she starts trolling the crowd for witnesses. Unless you're ready to explain why you're sneaking around her crime scene uninvited."

Daniel wasn't. "Good to see you, Frank."

Frank just gave a curt nod and strode back down the shallow incline toward the cordoned-off crime scene.

Daniel waited until Frank had slipped under the yellow tape before he followed, skirting the crowd again to keep his distance from the cops and technicians still swarming the crime scene. It was possible someone might recognize his face from his TV appearances.

Daniel wasn't ready for that to happen. Not yet.

Not until he knew if these murders really were connected to Tina Carter's.

He settled behind the wheel of his Jeep, his attention focused on the police officers on the scene. Sooner or later, detectives would head for the victim's home, looking for a murder scene that would provide them with more evidence than the carefully staged dumpsite they were scouring at the moment.

And when they did, Daniel intended to tag along.

THE BROOKSTONE APARTMENTS on Doberville Road had been built in the twenties, a redbrick Colonial Georgian the owner had partitioned into apartments years ago when apartment housing in Birmingham's vibrant Southside community had become a hot-ticket item. Alice's apartment was on the backside of the building, making it easy for Rose to approach from the alley without attracting much attention.

She climbed the exterior stairs, the memory of the death veil quivering over Alice's face haunting her. She should have made Alice believe her. Maybe if she'd come across matter-of-fact, less uncertain…

Maybe, maybe, maybe. Maybe Alice just had a bad hangover and had overslept. No need to give up hope yet.

But her loud raps on Alice's door brought no response. "Alice, are you in there?"

No answer.

Panic built in her belly, coiling like snakes. "Alice, please come to the door!"

Rose pressed her ear to the door, listening. She felt the hum of electricity against her cheek and the faint sound of voices coming from other apartments, but from inside Alice's apartment, all was silent.

Frustrated, she followed the wraparound balcony to the side of the building. Alice had a corner apartment with a side window; maybe she could see through the curtains.

As she approached the window, movement at the front of the building distracted her. Two cars, one of them a marked police cruiser, pulled up the drive, heading for the parking lot at the back.

Rose flattened herself against the side of the building, her heart in her throat. The police were here because of Alice. And not just because the woman at the flower shop had called them, either.

They would only be here this quickly if they'd already found Alice's body.

The police cars disappeared around the building. In a few seconds they'd come back into view. Rose didn't intend to be here waiting for them. She knew better than to try to explain death veils to the police. She'd tried telling the Willow Grove police about what she'd seen in Dillon's face when she had reported the Granvilles' deaths. They'd practically accused her of lying—and those policemen had known her since she was a baby.

The Birmingham police didn't know her from Adam. They wouldn't hesitate to make her their prime suspect.

She raced for the stairs, making it to the first-floor breezeway unseen. She darted across the lawn and descended the steep driveway to the street. She headed down the sidewalk, keeping her gaze on the road ahead. If she looked back, she'd only attract more attention.

She should never have told the woman at the flower shop her name. The police would surely speak to Alice's coworkers and, if the woman on the phone remembered Rose's name—

She turned at the corner and headed uphill toward home, her breath coming in short huffs. Ignoring a stitch in her side, she took the concrete steps to her house two at a time.

"What are you running from?"

A man's voice jarred up her spine. She stumbled, grabbing for the iron railing to keep from falling, and whirled around, her muscles bunching, prepared for fight or flight.

The dark-haired man from the pub the night before stood just feet away, his expression tinged with curiosity. His gaze swept over her, through her, as if he were studying every atom, every cell, every drop of blood coursing through her veins.

"What do you want?" she asked.

"Saw you last night. At the Southside Pub."

"If you don't leave now I'm going to call the police."

His lips curved. "Should be easy. They're only a block away."

Her heart skipped another beat. "Who are you?"

"Daniel. Who are you?"

She pressed her lips together and took a step backward up the stairs. "You're trespassing on private property."

"You were at the home of a murder victim. Why?"

She tightened her grip on the railing. "I don't know what you're talking about."

"The police are knocking on her door right now to see if anyone else is home. You ran when you saw them coming. Why?"

Rather than answer, she turned and started up the steps.

He followed, his footfalls thudding close behind. "Was she your friend?"

She made it to the porch and turned to face him from above. "If you don't leave now, I will call the police."

He stopped, gazing up at her, a challenge in his smoky eyes. "Be my guest."

She turned and went inside, slamming the door behind her. She flipped the dead bolt and rested her head against the heavy wood door, her heart fluttering with panic.

Who was he? Alice's killer, coming here to taunt her? Whoever had been hiding in the shadows at the end of the side parking lot had seen her.

Had he chosen her as his next victim, after all?

Crossing the foyer on shaky legs, she peered at herself in the antique mirror over the narrow hall table. Her haunted expression gazed back at her, pale and wide-eyed but free of any sort of phantom veil.

Her legs felt boneless. She made it to the living room before her knees buckled. She fell gracelessly onto the sofa, slumping forward, her head in her hands.

If the gray-eyed man was the killer—and, really, why couldn't he be?—he wasn't what she'd expected. She'd imagined that a man who could brutalize a woman the way the killer had done must have some mark of evil, a coldness in the gaze or a cruelty around the mouth that would tell her "he's the one."

Rationally, she knew it didn't work that way. The nice man who lived next door and kept his lawn mowed and his house painted could turn out to be the most twisted of killers, and nobody would have a clue. But she *should* have a clue. For whatever reason, she'd been saddled with this terrifying ability to foresee death. She should damned well be able to spot a killer.

For the past few months she'd been stumbling around in dark, feeling her way through a maze of sharp edges and dizzying pitfalls. As if witnessing Dillon Granville's suicide had struck her blind, robbed her of the true-love veils and left her with a cruel facsimile, the death veils that now haunted her day and night.

Nearby, her cell phone trilled. She was tempted to ignore it, let the caller leave a message, but she had a business to run, bills to pay. It was probably Melissa with a question about the caterer or the floral arrangements—

Melissa. She had no idea Alice was dead.

By the time she found her cell phone, the ringing had stopped. The number on the display window belonged to her sister, Iris. She was leaving a message.

Rose crossed to the front door as she waited for the message indicator to show up on her cell phone, peering through the narrow glass panel to the right of the door. Rose saw no sign of the man who'd called himself Daniel.

The message light on her cell phone began to blink. She pressed the button, knowing what she'd hear. It had been almost two weeks since she'd last spoken to Iris, and her sister wasn't used to being an outsider in Rose's life.

"Rose, are you ignoring my calls?" Iris's light tone couldn't hide the dark current of hurt. "Lily's thinking about hosting Thanksgiving dinner at her house. She said she and Casey are already planning a menu."

Casey was her sister Lily's stepdaughter. Lily's visions had helped reunite Casey with her father, police lieutenant J. McBride. Lily'd fallen in love with the gruff cop in the process, marrying him not long after Casey's return.

Rose had known Lily would marry McBride from the start. A true-love veil had told her so.

Dashing away tears with her fingertips, she started to dial the phone, resolved to call Iris and commit to being there for Thanksgiving. But another memory stopped her, a flash of shimmery silver slashed with deep crimson, hovering over Alice Donovan's pretty features.

Iris and Lily knew she'd lost her ability to see true-love veils, but she hadn't yet told them about the death veils. Even the thought of telling them made her cringe. The death veils made her feel dirty, stained by the miscalculation that had led to Carrie Granville's death and Dillon's suicide.

She shut off her phone, fresh tears of despair spilling down her cheeks. She didn't know how to tell Iris or Lily what was wrong with her. She couldn't find the words to explain how upside down her life had become since that nightmarish Christmas Eve in Bridey Woods.

A few months ago she'd moved her business and her life to Birmingham, where everyone was a stranger and nobody knew about true-love veils, Carrie and Dillon Granville or the fact that the nice wedding planner in the pretty old Southside house could tell them they were going to die within the next month.

Everything was different now. *She* was different.

The death veils had built an impenetrable wall between her and the two people she loved most in the world, and she didn't know how to tear it down.

DANIEL COULD HAVE afforded a top-of-the-line hotel but had opted for an economy motel just outside the city, where he'd be left alone to pore over his files and notes uninterrupted. He'd had another option, of course; he could have gone home. His mother still lived in the same cozy Tudor in Forest Park where he'd spent his childhood.

His brother, Evan, a doctor, lived south of town with his beautiful wife and two children under the age of three. They kept an eye on his mother, made sure she was keeping up with old friends and doctor visits and not sinking into loneliness.

She was lucky to have Evan and his family. God knows what she'd do if Daniel was all she had to depend on.

Guilt tugged at the back of his neck, a familiar feeling. He had a lot to answer for where his family was concerned, and all he'd accomplished over the past decade wasn't enough to erase the trouble he'd been when he was younger.

He'd stop by to check on her before he left town.

Meanwhile, he had the name of victim number three, thanks to his mystery woman. She'd knocked on the door of apartment 2-D. All he'd had to do was call up the address in a reverse directory and he had the name. Alice Donovan. A quick Internet search had connected her to a flower shop on Twentieth Street. He made a note in his day planner to stop by the place later that afternoon, see if the other employees could help him flesh out who she was and how she might have ended up at the mercy of a killer.

He'd had less luck with the dark-haired woman he'd seen at the pub the night before. He had her address now, but the reverse directory updated once a year. Apparently she'd moved into the house on Mountain Avenue less than a year ago.

He let it go, for now. Steve, his teaching assistant, had e-mailed some new information that needed his attention.

Steve had attached three new articles, two from Tennessee and one from Arkansas, all dated between six and nine months earlier. They filled in a gap between the Colbert County murders and the Texas murders he'd documented last year.

The killer he'd informally dubbed Orion, after the hunter in mythology, seemed to move around a lot. From job to job? Or did his job allow him to travel widely and at will? It was a question Daniel hadn't yet answered to his own satisfaction. A traveling salesman would make a lot of sense, considering how widespread the murders were. But his crimes also seemed to indicate a certain level of trust on the part of his victims—he couldn't have killed so many women without being caught if women were wary about him.

Maybe there wasn't just one killer. Maybe he was

all wrong and Orion was a series of different killers with similar M.O.s and signatures. It was possible, wasn't it?

Maybe he was seeing what he wanted to see, putting together patterns that didn't really exist because he needed those patterns to take shape and make sense of a mystery he'd been trying to solve for the past thirteen years.

Daniel scrubbed his hands over his gritty eyes, thinking back to the shock of seeing Frank Carter at the crime scene that morning. His memory of Tina's brother was little more than a series of snapshots frozen in time: Frank watching from the stairs as Daniel picked up Tina for a college formal. Frank eyeing Daniel's new Firebird with all the hungry interest of a fifteen-year-old with a learner's permit burning a hole in the pocket of his Levi's.

Frank's dark, tragic eyes as he watched the shiny silver casket being lowered into the grave bearing a simple gray stone marked with his sister's name.

Did Frank see the similarities? The telltale slash marks, the obscene pose mimicking peaceful death? Surely, he did. How could he not?

He wondered, with envy, if Frank had been able to let go of that one violence-stained moment of his life and move on. Maybe he didn't spend his free time obsessing on crime stats and police reports, looking for those key similarities that might suggest Tina's killer was still out there, still taking lives.

Still catchable.

Good for him if he didn't. Good for him if he could close his eyes at night and sleep in peace. Daniel couldn't.

He hadn't slept peacefully in thirteen years.

MELISSA BANNERMAN slumped in the armchair across from Rose, her expression stunned. "Someone murdered her? Last night?"

Rose nodded.

"My God." Tears welled up in Melissa's eyes, spilling down her cheeks. "Oh, my God."

"I hate being the one to have to tell you—"

"How did you find out?"

"I heard it on the radio, just before you got here." The two o'clock news report had finally confirmed what Rose had already known. Alice Donovan was dead.

"My God. Her poor parents." Melissa shook her head.

"I called the flower shop this morning like I said I would," Rose added. It was the truth, if an incomplete version. "The woman who answered was obviously upset when I asked for Alice. I managed to get her to tell me that Alice hadn't shown up at work on time and they couldn't reach her at home."

"She lives only a block from here." Melissa wiped her cheeks, her expression slack and numb.

"I'd gotten that out of her employee. I went to check, but the police had arrived, and I'd thought it best to get out of the way."

"Was she in her apartment?"

"The news reports don't say."

"She just had a new alarm system put in her apartment. I told her it was overkill, but there've been two murders in the neighborhood recently, and she didn't feel safe." Melissa sniffled. "God, what about funeral arrangements?"

"I imagine there'll be some delay, given the circumstances. Give her family time to process everything, and they'll be in touch, I'm sure." Rose took a deep breath. "Will you let me know when you get the details? I'd like to pay my respects."

That wasn't the truth; she could think of a million things she'd rather do than attend Alice Donovan's funeral. But she knew in her bones that *he'd* be there. The one who'd killed her.

So she had to be there, too.

"The other murders—they were both young women, too, weren't they?" Melissa asked.

"Yes." Sherry Nicholson had been twenty-eight, Elisa Biondi twenty-six. Both had lived in Southside and both had been to Southside bars within a day or two of their deaths.

"I don't want to think about my wedding today." Melissa stood and wiped her eyes. "It's too cruel, thinking happy thoughts today. I'll call Monday and we'll regroup from there."

Rose saw her out, watching from the doorway until she was safely to her car in Rose's driveway. As Melissa backed her Lexus onto Mountain Avenue, Rose started to close the door.

Until she caught sight of the blue sedan across the street.

A ripple of unease fluttered through her. The windows of the car were tinted dark, but she could make out the shape of someone in the driver's seat.

Heart thudding, she went back inside the house and locked the door behind her, taking deep breaths to calm herself.

It could be nothing. A salesman between appointments, pulled over to talk on his cell phone. Someone considering one of the empty apartments dotted along Mountain Avenue.

Or the man who'd accosted her this morning on her way back from Alice's.

She peered out the tall, narrow window that flanked the door, hoping the bright daylight would hide her from view.

The sedan was gone.

She slumped against the wall, not sure whether to be relieved or alarmed.

HIS HEART POUNDED a swift, steady cadence, blood rushing in his ears. He always felt energized after he took his prey, but this time was different in an entirely unexpected way.

Because of her.

The pretty brunette who'd tried to warn Alice that she was going to die.

He hadn't planned to kill sweet Alice last night. He'd noticed her when she arrived at the club, her wavy dark hair spilling around her shoulders in soft waves. Pretty in an obvious way, she'd fascinated him with her reckless need to dance off whatever was bothering her. He'd fantasized about the first cut, the blood trickling over her pink cheeks and down into the cleft between her full breasts. But he hadn't planned to kill her. Until he'd heard the other woman's warning.

"I see death."

Somehow, she'd known, even before he'd made his selection. She'd known that Alice was the one.

When she'd showed up outside Alice's apartment this morning, he'd known for certain that something special was happening.

He'd found his muse.

Chapter Three

"I'd like to see Ms. Bannerman," Daniel said.

The receptionist, a motherly-looking woman in her midforties, arched one eyebrow as she read the business card he'd handed her. "Do you have an appointment?"

"No. I was in the area when I had the idea I'd like to discuss with her, so I thought I'd drop in to see if she had a moment to speak with me." Daniel smiled at the woman, hoping a little charm might nudge her toward buzzing her boss.

"I'll see if she's available." The receptionist looked pointedly toward the brown-leather wing-backed chairs in the waiting area. Daniel retreated to one of them, taking a look around the office of Bannerman and Bannerman Publishing.

It was a converted loft on Morris Avenue; unlikely digs for a publishing company that had been in business for more than a hundred years. The Bannermans were old money and lots of it, but apparently the new generation was dragging the company kicking and screaming into the new millennium.

A few minutes with the distraught—and talkative—

employees at Five Points Floral Creations Monday morning had led Daniel to Alice Donovan's college friend, Melissa. Alice and Melissa had gone clubbing Friday night. Melissa might well have been the last person to see Alice alive besides her killer.

Luckily, with a couple of bestsellers under his belt, Daniel had a good excuse to call on Alice's grieving friend.

He didn't enjoy taking advantage of her vulnerability, but it was a necessary evil. She might have information about the man who'd killed Alice and a lot of other women. So when the receptionist informed him Ms. Bannerman could spare him a couple of moments, he buried his guilt and headed for her office.

Melissa Bannerman was a pretty blonde in her late twenties, dressed in an expensive gray suit with a pale green blouse, which flattered her tall, lithe build. Recent attempts to repair her makeup couldn't hide her tear-reddened eyes or the shell-shocked expression beneath the practiced smile. When she shook his hand, her grip was firm, but he felt the faintest underlying tremor. "It's a pleasure to meet you, Dr. Hartman. I've read all your books and enjoyed them immensely."

"Glad to hear it." Daniel sat in the chair she indicated. "I'm here in town doing some research on a cold case, and that's when I had the idea for a new book. I'm between publishers, and the idea I have is ideally suited to a boutique publishing house like this one, so I thought I'd give you my pitch to see what you think."

Melissa's blue eyes narrowed slightly. "I can't imagine a larger publisher wouldn't jump at the chance to publish any book you chose to write."

"Maybe, but I've heard good things about Bannerman."

Her smile almost made it to her eyes. "What's your idea?"

"Cases in the South that have never been solved."

A flicker of pain darted across her face. "Intriguing."

Daniel leaned forward. "Something's wrong, isn't it? I came at a bad time."

Her expression started to crumble. Tears glistened in her eyes. She caught herself before she broke into tears, but her lower lip quivered as she replied, "No, of course not."

"I can tell you're upset. Can I get you a glass of water?"

His kindness seemed to do her in. The tears spilled over, streaking her cheeks. "I lost a friend on Friday and I just got off the phone with her parents."

"Sorry to hear it. Was it sudden?"

Grief lined her pretty face. "She was murdered."

As Daniel gently led her to tell him more details about the night of Alice's murder, the story spilled from her in a rush of sadness and rage.

"Alice left the club around ten or so. She said she had an early morning. I'd have gone with her, but Rose was still there."

"Rose?"

"Rose Browning, my wedding planner." Melissa fluttered her left hand, showing off a large diamond solitaire. "We ran into her at Sizzle. She was still there when Alice left, so I stayed. Only, then Rose left about a minute after Alice."

"So Rose might have seen Alice outside?"

Melissa's brow wrinkled. "You sound like a cop."

"Occupational hazard. Have you talked to the police yet?"

"Yes. I don't know much, but maybe it'll help track her movements that night, right?"

"Has your friend Rose talked to the police?"

"I don't know. I'll ask her tomorrow at the funeral."

"Obviously, this isn't a good time to discuss my idea." He rose and handed her his card. "In a week or so, give me a call." Though he'd used the book idea to get in the door, he'd been contemplating it for a while. He'd give Melissa a fair chance to make a good offer. Meanwhile, he needed to talk to Rose Browning, preferably before she talked to the police.

As Melissa walked him to the door, he asked, "Your wedding planner—you don't happen to have her card, do you?"

"Somewhere around here. Are you in the market?"

"Maybe." He smiled at her.

"She's easy to find—she lives in a big brick Colonial Georgian on Mountain Avenue. It's 601 Mountain Avenue—right on the corner. You can't miss it."

He didn't react outwardly, but his heartbeat quickened. He knew the house she was talking about. And now he knew the name of his mystery woman. All that was left was to figure out what to do with the information.

SERENITY RIDGE CEMETERY stretched across rolling green hills just outside the Birmingham city limits. Granite and marble gravestones lined the hills like soldiers in formation, waiting for their marching orders.

Tina Carter's grave lay in the far eastern corner of the cemetery, close to the access road. Fall leaves cov-

ered the fading grass and the base of the marble headstone. By the gravestone, a small urn of faded silk roses
lay overturned.

Daniel set the urn upright, adding the arrangement
he'd picked up at Alice Donovan's flower shop that
morning. If Tina's mother was still alive, the grave
would be immaculately tended, he knew. Fresh flowers
left daily, the leaves swept from the headstone and the
grass cut above Tina's silent resting place.

But Mary Frances Carter had died earlier that year
of a heart attack and, apparently, Frank still couldn't
bring himself to visit his sister's grave after all these
years.

Daniel brushed the leaves away from the grave,
something Frank had said thirteen years earlier still
vivid in his memory. It had been the day of Tina's
funeral, moments after the final prayer. Frank had
been standing next to Daniel, tears trembling in his red-
dened eyes. "I can't stand to even walk by her room anymore," he'd confessed as cemetery workers had lowered
the casket into the ground. "Mama's made it into a
shrine."

Poor Frank. Tina had always been their mother's
favorite, more so after her death. Emotionally, Mary
Frances had left her teenage son to his own devices, too
wrapped up in grief for the child she'd lost to deal with
the child left behind.

A glass-encased photo of Tina hung over the in-
scription on her tombstone, her pretty smile captured for
eternity on a face that would never grow old. Her eyes
glowed with life.

Daniel pulled his handkerchief from his pocket and

polished the glass. Twenty-one and beautiful forever, he thought.

Only, she hadn't been beautiful at the end. Her killer had marred that porcelain skin with slashes and gouges with his rage. He'd slit her throat, silencing her soft voice.

Daniel rose, gazing down at the tombstone. *Did Orion kill you, too, Tina? Am I finally going to find him this time?*

Tina's grave lay silent, offering no answers.

Daniel turned and walked back toward the funeral home barely visible at the far end of the cemetery grounds. Today, another woman would be laid to rest, her life silenced by the slashes and strokes of a killer's rage.

And, if Daniel was lucky, Orion would show up to see what sorrow his handiwork had created.

ROSE SMOOTHED the lapel of her dark brown suit and studied her reflection in the Impala's driver's side window. She looked sober and nondescript, she noted with satisfaction, her dark hair tucked into a simple knot at the base of her neck and her makeup at a minimum.

She'd come to Alice's funeral to see, not be seen.

She spotted Melissa Bannerman and her fiancé, Mark Phagan, just inside the foyer of the Serenity Ridge Funeral Home. Melissa was simply incapable of blending into her surroundings, despite the conservative lines of her navy suit. Pulling her blond hair into a straight ponytail only emphasized her fashion-model cheekbones and cornflower-blue eyes. She was as tall as Mark, towering over most of the women and half the men in the foyer, drawing the eyes of every red-blooded male in the place regardless of the somber occasion.

Melissa's gaze connected with Rose's. She waved Rose over. "You remember Mark, don't you?"

Mark managed a pained smile, obviously wishing he were anywhere else.

Rose followed Melissa into the small chapel, where Alice's coffin took up the front. They found a pew in the middle, Mark entering first, leaving Rose on the aisle. Melissa inclined her head toward a sandy-haired man sitting by himself a couple of rows up. "That's Richard Hughes, Alice's ex."

The man Alice had been drinking and dancing to forget, Rose thought. She watched him, wondering if he could have been the figure in the shadows. The police had probably questioned him already—significant others were always the first suspects in any murder investigation. Was he still on their list?

Melissa and Mark seemed to know most of the mourners in the chapel. Understandable; funerals were often like reunions, bringing together people who hadn't seen each other in years. Melissa, Alice and Mark had all attended Alabama together, and many of the people in the tiny chapel shared that common past.

Just not Rose.

For most of her life, that wouldn't have mattered. "Never met a stranger and never will," her sister Lily used to tease.

But Rose wasn't that person anymore.

She gritted her teeth against the creeping sense of self-consciousness and glanced at the growing crowd filling the pews behind her, letting her gaze move smoothly from face to face without settling long enough to attract unwanted attention. The man standing in the back of the chapel looked familiar; it took a moment to place him as Detective Carter, the policeman who'd taken her statement on Monday after Alice's murder. If he recognized her, he gave no indication.

Rose started to turn back around when her gaze settled on a tall, lean man in a charcoal suit entering the back door of the chapel. Her heart seized.

It was the man who'd accosted her outside her house the day after Alice's murder. The one named Daniel.

He met her gaze, his eyes narrowing briefly. He inclined his head in silent greeting as he slid into one of the back pews.

Rose faced forward, her heart racing. Who was he? Why was he here? The skin on the back of her neck prickled. Was he looking at her, even now?

She leaned toward Melissa. "Do you see the man at the back of the chapel, wearing a dark gray suit with a blue-and-gray striped tie?"

Melissa glanced over her shoulder. Her eyebrows arched. "You mean, Daniel Hartman? Weird. Wonder why he's here."

"You know him?"

"Yes. He's a famous profiler. Used to be with the FBI. He's a professor or something now. Haven't you ever heard of him? He's always on the true-crime programs on TV, talking about this case or that." She lowered her voice. "I'm considering publishing a new book of his."

As the funeral director took the podium and began the service, Rose slumped in the pew, mulling the new information. She barely heard any of the eulogy, her earlier tension fading into annoyance as she realized just how many hours over the past couple of days she'd spent in fear of her mystery man, when he could have eased her worries with a simple introduction.

After the service, Melissa turned to her. "I need to talk to her parents for a minute. Are you going to the graveside for the rest of the service?"

Rose shook her head. She'd had enough of death for today. "I'll call you tomorrow and we can get back to planning your wedding. Happier things, right?"

Melissa gave her a quick hug. "Thanks for coming."

Rose stood, stealing the opportunity to glance at the pew where she'd last seen Daniel. He was no longer there.

She looked around the chapel, trying to spot him in the milling crowd heading for the exit, but she couldn't find him. She did spot Detective Carter again and, for a moment, she considered flagging him down to tell him about Daniel. The police might want to know they had a rogue profiler sniffing around their case.

But telling Detective Carter about Daniel meant admitting she'd been at Alice's apartment the morning she'd turned up dead, a piece of information Rose had withheld from the detective during their brief interview a couple of days earlier.

He'd want to know why she'd run away when the police showed up. And the only answer that made sense was the one she had no intention of giving. Detective Carter had seemed the open-minded, reasonable sort, but she wasn't about to tell a cop that she had foreseen the deaths of three of the slasher's victims.

She joined the mourners heading for the exit, peeling off when she reached the foyer to find a restroom. Spotting the signs at the other end of the foyer, she started weaving her way through the crowd.

Halfway there, the sound of Mark Phagan's smooth baritone caught her ear. "It's no big deal—I just had other stuff to do—but Melissa thinks I was with y'all at the game. So if it comes up, that's where I was, okay?"

Rose followed his voice and found Mark standing a few feet away, addressing a couple of men who looked to be around his age. Both men nodded, one shooting a wry half-grin at the other as if sharing a private joke.

Rose's heart sank. Mark had already cheated at least once during the engagement. Was he doing it again?

She gave herself a mental shake and pushed on toward the restrooms. Whether Mark was cheating or not, that was for Melissa to figure out by herself. The last time Rose had tried to interfere with the course of true love, her efforts had ended in tragedy in the middle of Bridey Woods.

The restroom was full, women waiting in single file along the wall for their turn inside. Rose fell in behind the last woman, letting her gaze wander to the opposite wall where a bulletin board hung next to the door of the business office. Amid a sea of white sheets of paper full of tiny black type, a sunny yellow flyer gleamed like a beacon, catching her eye.

Special Neighborhood Meeting, read the bold

headline across the top of the page. Below, an announcement of free CPR lessons listed a date and time. Too bad it wasn't self-defense lessons instead, Rose thought.

She cocked her head. Why couldn't it be? Why couldn't the Southside neighborhood association set up a special meeting, bring in the police or a self-defense expert to tell women how to avoid being the killer's next victim? The women in the neighborhood weren't receiving any warning at all. The police weren't putting suspect sketches on the evening news or even admitting that the killings were connected—didn't want to "panic" people.

But if the neighborhood association got involved, the police wouldn't have much choice, would they? Get enough voices clamoring for answers, and the police might have to admit what Rose already knew: There was a killer stalking Southside and, if he wasn't stopped, more women would die.

She had the association president's contact information filed somewhere at home. She'd call as soon as she got there.

DANIEL WAS WAITING in the funeral-home foyer when Frank Carter emerged from the chapel. His old friend met his gaze with a wry half-smile. "Imagine meeting you here."

"Just thinking of you a little while ago," Daniel said. "Stopped by Tina's grave on the way in."

Frank's expression darkened. "See any ghosts?"

Not quite the response Daniel expected. "Only the ones in my mind. Still avoiding the place?"

Frank didn't answer.

"Meant to tell you, I was sorry to hear about your mother," Daniel added. "Mom wrote to tell me about it."

"It was strange. She was in good health all the way up to the massive coronary. I don't know, maybe if I'd been here, I might have seen the signs." He shrugged. "Ten years away, and the first time I come back home, it's to bury my mother."

"And decided to stay?"

"Something like that."

"Where are you living these days?"

"Home sweet home," Frank said with a grimace. "The place needs a lot of work before it's ready to sell and I don't see the point of spending rent money on an apartment when the house is there and paid for."

"Shrine still there?" Daniel asked.

Frank's scowl answered the question. "I still can't go in there. I know it sounds crazy, but it's like she's still there. I just…can't."

"Going to make it hard to sell the house."

Frank slanted a look at Daniel. "I'm working up to it." He moved ahead, toward the exit to join the mourners lining up for the slow drive out to the newly turned grave at the far side of the cemetery.

Daniel lingered behind, looking for Rose Browning. He'd kept an eye out for her since spotting her heading toward the restrooms. He hadn't seen her come out, so she had to still be back there somewhere.

Unless there was a rear exit.

As he started toward the corridor, the object of his search emerged, stopping short as her startled gaze met his.

"I'm not going to hurt you," he said quietly.

She narrowed her eyes. "I didn't think you were."

"I need to talk to you."

One dark eyebrow arched. "About what?"

"Alice Donovan's murder."

The other eyebrow lifted. "Why would I want to talk to you about Alice's murder? You're not a policeman."

He debated telling her who he was and why he was interested, but he didn't want to lay out all his cards yet. He compromised. "Actually, I'm something of a true-crime buff. I'm thinking about writing a book on un-solved murders in the southeast."

"You want to write about people murdering other people?"

Not the question he'd expected. "Maybe what I write will help solve the crimes."

Her pale brown eyes glittered with skepticism. "Right."

He couldn't blame her for her doubt. It wasn't a great cover story but it had the advantage of being the truth. Sort of. "Whoever killed Alice has killed before."

She didn't look surprised. Interesting.

"There was another woman about a month ago. Sher-ry Nicholson. Seen leaving the Anchor on Magnolia Avenue around midnight. Next morning her body turned up in the woods near Vulcan Park." When Rose didn't respond, he continued. "Victim number two was a med student at U.A.B."

"Elisa Biondi," Rose blurted softly.

He narrowed his eyes. "Yes."

"They're connected, aren't they?"

"I think so."

Her gaze lifted to meet his. "Interesting hobby you have."

He didn't like her cool tone. What he did wasn't a hobby; it was his job. He was damned good at it. Sometimes he got a big rush out of it. A lot of women found him fascinating because of what he chose to do with his life. Just not Rose Browning, apparently.

"He didn't start here in Birmingham," he said.

Her brow creased. "You think he's killed before?"

Daniel hesitated, not sure why he'd opened up to her as much as he had already. He needed to control the conversation, not get sucked into spilling his guts to a big-eyed brunette beauty with her own secrets. "Why were you at Alice Donovan's the other morning?"

She hesitated before answering. "I called her business that morning, and her employees were worried because she was very late. I'd offered to check on her. What were you doing there?"

"Following the police from the crime scene."

She gave a soft huff of surprised laughter.

"I talked to your client, Melissa Bannerman. She told me you were at a club with her and Alice the night she died. Said you left a minute or so after Alice."

Rose cocked her head. "Melissa told you that?"

"Yes."

She stepped back, putting more distance between them. "Or maybe you were stalking Alice."

He ignored the accusation. "Did you see Alice leave?"

"Yes. I saw her drive away, and she was alone and fine." Rose started to walk briskly toward the exit.

Daniel caught up with her outside the funeral home. "That's all you saw?"

"You think I saw someone grab her and just forgot to call the police?" She pinned him with a fierce glare.

"You may have seen something you don't realize you saw."

"I didn't," she said. But unease flickered over her face.

"Maybe someone at the bar paying too much attention to her. Or a car that left the parking lot right after hers—"

"I didn't see anything like that." She moved away, heading toward the parking lot. He let her go, walking to his Jeep at a more leisurely pace. She was already pulling out onto the highway by the time he slid behind the steering wheel.

No matter. He knew where she lived.

"Is IT A GO?" Rose tightened her grip on her cell phone, waiting for the neighborhood association president's response.

"Tuesday at seven, regular room," John Fielding answered.

Rose sighed with relief. "Perfect. Do you need me to help pass out the fliers?"

"We'll have some printed up by one o'clock this afternoon. You can pick up a batch then." He gave her the address of his law firm.

"I'll be there." Rose hung up and looked across the desk at Melissa Bannerman. "It's on—next Tuesday at seven."

Melissa smiled, though sadness lingered in her eyes. "I can't believe you got it put together so quickly."

"It wasn't me, it was Mr. Fielding. He even managed to get the police to cooperate."

Melissa looked surprised. "Did you think they wouldn't?"

"The guy's killed three women, and the cops haven't got a clue. That's not something they like to talk about."

"Well, I definitely plan to be there." Melissa stood, picking up the suit jacket draped over her desk chair. "After what happened to Alice, I've decided there's no such thing as being too careful. I have a technician coming first thing in the morning to put in a new alarm system."

"That's probably a good idea," Rose agreed. She should consider it herself, although money was tight at the moment.

Melissa shrugged on her jacket and motioned toward the door. "Let's go see what the Elegant Eatery has to offer."

Rose let Melissa take the lead at the caterer's, knowing her strong-willed client would make her own decision regardless of what Rose might suggest. She was too keyed up to sample the goods, anyway.

She couldn't stop thinking about what Daniel Hartman had told her at Alice's funeral.

It had been bad enough knowing that the killer had murdered three women. But if Daniel was right, he'd killed dozens of women across several states without being caught.

How could she possibly stop him before he killed again?

Chapter Four

A black ribbon still hung on the door of Five Points Floral Creations when Daniel arrived after lunchtime the Friday after Alice Donovan's funeral. He recognized the clerk he'd met on Monday when he'd stopped by to find out more about Alice's movements the night she'd died.

Daniel avoided the clerk, taking a slow tour of the display area, looking for a fall arrangement to send to his mother. A week in town and still he hadn't called her.

He was a lousy son.

He took a bouquet of fall asters to the cashier's counter where the clerk, a pretty girl with short black hair and a sapphire nose stud, met him with a smile. Sasha, he remembered.

She recognized him, as well. "Hi. Daniel, right? Did you get in touch with Ms. Bannerman?"

He handed her his credit card. "I did, thanks."

"I hope you can help find out who killed Alice. I still can't get my mind around it." Sasha handed him his receipt.

"Do you know Ms. Browning, too?"

Sasha's brow wrinkled. "Ms. Browning?"

"She's a wedding planner. Talked to someone here on the phone the morning Alice…" He let the words trail, watching for her reaction.

"Oh, the one who offered to check on Alice." Sasha's eyes widened with sudden horror. "Was she the one who found her?"

Behind them, the bell above the door jingled again. Daniel turned to find the subject of his questions entering the store, her dark hair pulled back in a severe twist, her slim body clad in a conservative gray suit. But she still exuded a sort of wild, natural beauty that made his heart skip a beat.

Her light brown eyes locked with his. "Daniel."

"Ms. Browning."

She looked at the floral arrangement in front of him on the counter, a question in her eyes. He ignored the silent query and looked down at her hands, which held a sheaf of bright yellow paper. Large black capital letters spanned the top of the papers: Protect Yourself.

Daniel reached for the top sheet, ignoring Rose's glare.

"Southside Neighborhood Association Special Meeting. Tuesday evening at 7:00 p.m." The date and location were listed, along with Frank Carter's name—he was to speak to the attendees about self-protection.

Daniel looked at Rose, whose glare was both angry and defensive. Did she expect him to scoff? "It's a good idea."

"Something needs to be done," she answered tightly. After a brief pause she added, "You're welcome to attend, of course."

He tamped down a smile of amusement at her grudging offer. "I'll check my schedule."

She moved past him, handing several flyers to Sasha. "Could you put a few of these where your customers can see them and pick up a copy? We're trying to get the word out."

Sasha took the flyers. "Of course."

Rose turned back to Daniel, her chin coming up again as if in self-defense. She handed him one of the flyers. "In case your schedule is clear."

He folded the paper and slipped it in his pocket, his gaze following her as she left the shop and headed down the sidewalk toward the next store. A neighborhood meeting was actually a damned good idea. He should have thought of it himself. A killer couldn't move as easily in places where the citizens were informed and alert.

Orion's decision to kill in a smaller area made him more vulnerable, and this meeting might even draw him out. Could a smart, experienced killer really resist the chance to see his potential victims all in one place?

Daniel was pretty sure the answer was no. Orion would be at the meeting Tuesday night. Daniel knew it deep in his gut.

And he'd be waiting for him.

THE LIBRARY meeting room was already starting to fill up by the time Rose arrived Tuesday evening with her contribution to the refreshments table, a tin of apple-bran minimuffins. As she was placing them on a platter, Melissa Bannerman arrived with a box of pastries from the Elegant Eatery.

"Oh, good, I was afraid I'd be late!" Melissa set the

pastries next to Rose's tray and folded the box top to display the confections. She dusted powdered sugar off her fingers and looked around the room. "Nice crowd."

"People are worried—"

Melissa's attention fixed on someone across the room. "Hey, there's Jesse."

Rose followed her gaze. A sandy-haired man in a white button-down shirt and jeans stood near the doorway. He spotted Melissa and smiled, nodding in her direction.

"Jesse?" Rose murmured, arching an eyebrow.

Melissa made a face at her. "The technician who put in my new alarm system. He's with Professional Security Systems. You should give them a call. Jesse!" Melissa waved the man over.

He crossed to them, his smile spreading over his face. "Melissa! It's nice to see you again."

The familiarity in his tone surprised Rose. He spoke as if Melissa was an intimate friend rather than a client. Though in fairness to him, Melissa was the type of person who never met a stranger. Maybe the security technician figured, when in Rome—

"Jesse Phillips, this is Rose Browning. You should give her your card. She might be in the market for a system."

Jesse produced a business card and smiled warmly. "Nice to meet you, Rose. Do you live in a house or an apartment?"

"House," she said, taking the card. His fingers brushed hers—deliberately, she suspected. She forced herself not to jerk her hand away. She glanced up at him again and found his gaze focused intently on her face.

"I love my new system," Melissa said. "A dozen levels of security but really user-friendly." Already her attention was straying, leaving Rose to deal with Jesse's laser focus.

"I bet you live in an old house," Jesse said, his voice pitched low. "I can tell you're an old soul." His gaze moved lazily over her, male appreciation glimmering in his eyes.

Rose had to wonder if she'd be so uneasy about his obvious interest in her if she hadn't lost the true-love veils. The old Rose loved to flirt, secure in the knowledge that, long before she got too involved with a man, the true-love veils would let her know whether or not he was the one for her.

But the veils were gone, leaving her off balance and wary of every man who looked her way. She couldn't deal with Jesse's obvious interest in her. She didn't know how, anymore. "I see someone I need to speak to." She started to move away.

Jesse caught her hand, his grip firm and hot, and gave it a quick shake. Her skin quivered uncomfortably where he touched her. "It was a delight to meet you. Give me a call and I'll set up an appointment and we'll get you a good system."

She managed a polite half smile as she began to weave her way through the crowd in search of the closest quiet corner. Before she made it halfway across the room, she ran headfirst into a solid wall of muscle.

"Excuse me—" She looked up, her apology dying in her throat as she stared up into Daniel Hartman's gunmetal eyes. "Daniel."

"Ms. Browning—"

"Rose, where'd you get off to—" Melissa came up behind Rose, stopping short when she saw Daniel. "Dr. Hartman."

"Good to see you again, Ms. Bannerman." Daniel glanced at Rose, no doubt wondering if she recognized his name. She feigned ignorance, wondering how much longer he planned to keep up his pretense. True-crime buff, indeed.

Melissa looked from Rose to Daniel and back, obviously aware of the tension stretching between them. "I guess you've met already. I told him about you."

Rose dragged her gaze away from Daniel's to look at Melissa. "You did?"

"He mentioned he was in the market for a wedding planner."

Rose slanted a look at Daniel.

His eyes glittered. "Thanks for the referral."

"We'd better grab a seat now if we want to be near the front." Melissa led the way to the front of the room, where there was a scattering of open seats. Melissa took one near the aisle and Rose settled in beside her.

Detective Carter entered the room and shook hands with the neighborhood association president. The detective exuded a sense of calm and purpose that eased the knot forming in Rose's stomach. Maybe his presentation would have the same effect on the jittery nerves of the women in the Southside neighborhood.

"Nice crowd." Daniel slipped into the empty chair next to Rose. He smelled good, as if he'd just stepped from the shower. Maybe he had; his dark hair had a hint of damp curl to it and a tiny nick on his jawline suggested a recent shave.

She pressed her lips together, annoyed at herself for noticing. "People around here are worried."

"With reason," he conceded.

Melissa leaned forward to look at Daniel. "Are you going to address the meeting, too?"

He shook his head. "Just here to observe."

"The presentation or the crowd?" Rose murmured.

Daniel met her curious gaze. "Both."

The look in his eyes sent the skin on the back of her neck crawling. Slowly, she turned to look at all the people settling into their seats behind her.

Her breath caught. Her heart skipped a beat and then hurtled headlong into hyperspeed.

Like a silvery sea of wraiths, almost every woman's face was covered with a blood-streaked death veil bearing the telltale ribbon of red across her throat.

The killer was here.

HE DRANK IN THE SIGHT of their faces, pale and dark, round and narrow, young and old. Apprehension and hope battled in their expressions, a sweet reminder of what his actions had created. They were his handiwork, these women teetering on the edge of panic. They feared his power and his whims.

It filled him with satisfaction, seeing them all gathered in neat little rows, awaiting words of comfort and hope.

How can we protect ourselves? What can we do to avoid becoming victims?

He hid a smile, kept his emotions in check. But inside, the answer rang in his head like an edict from on high.

Nothing.
Nothing.
Nothing.
They could do nothing to stop him now.

DANIEL HEARD Rose's soft intake of breath. He turned to find her looking at the crowd behind her, her face as pale as winter. He followed her haunted gaze. Had she seen someone? Did she know who Orion was? "What is it?"

Rose turned back to the front, her jaw rigid. "Nothing."

She was lying. She'd seen something. "What did you see?"

She pressed her pale lips together, not answering. But she looked terrified.

Daniel looked back over his shoulder, scanning the crowd. There were more women than men, although the crowd was liberally sprinkled with males, many of them there with their wives or girlfriends. Any one of them could be Orion; Daniel knew the killer he'd been tracking all these years had to be pretty damned good at blending in with average people or he wouldn't have escaped apprehension this long.

Was it the average Joe in the corner, sitting with his arm around a wide-eyed blonde with limp hair and baggy clothes? Was it the preppie-looking thirtysomething three rows back, wearing a bright green golf shirt, a trendy pair of Oakley sunglasses tucked into the breast pocket?

Who had Rose Browning seen that made her face go pale and her breathing shallow?

"Want something to drink?" he asked Rose.

She shook her head in the negative, but he got up and headed back to the refreshment table, anyway, determined to station himself along the wall by the time Frank started his presentation to the people gathered. There was no way in hell Orion could have resisted this meeting, and Daniel wanted to be in a position to observe the men in the audience. Something as simple as an inappropriate smile could betray the killer.

He kept his eye on the crowd as the neighborhood association president introduced Frank Carter and the topic of the evening. As John Fielding finished the introduction, he singled Rose out from the crowd, asking her to stand.

She stood, her expression placid but her red cheeks betraying her embarrassment. She glanced toward where Daniel leaned against the wall, and he gave a brief nod. Her color deepened and she quickly dropped back into her chair.

The neighborhood association president finished up and Frank took the podium. As he went into his presentation, Daniel pulled a notepad from his pocket and scanned the crowd.

By the time Frank finished giving a series of practical ways for women to protect themselves—safety in numbers, practicing radical awareness of one's surroundings, installing security devices for auto and home—Daniel had jotted notes on several men in the crowd whose behaviors had pinged his internal radar for odd behavior.

Unfortunately, none of them was Orion.

Still, there might be wife-beaters, rapists and con

artists in this crowd, and it wouldn't hurt to give Frank a heads-up.

After Frank's presentation ended, the crowd headed toward the back of the room to partake of the refreshments. Daniel scanned the crowd, looking for Rose Browning, but couldn't see her. Biting back a sigh of frustration, he headed for Carter.

"Everywhere I turn, there you are," Frank murmured, his voice desert-dry.

"Think your killer could resist a meeting like this?"

"You think it's the same guy for all three."

"He's killed other women in other places."

Frank's voice took on a different color. "Are you sure it's the *same* guy?"

Daniel met the detective's dark eyes. He knew they were talking about Tina's murder now. "Not yet."

Frank nodded. "Let me know if you figure it out."

"You'll be my first call."

"Did you notice any possibles?"

Daniel shook his head. "Not for Orion—"

"Orion?"

Daniel smiled, feeling a little self-conscious. "It's the name I've given him."

"Orion." Frank cocked his head. "I like it. It fits."

"Did see a few guys you should keep your eye on for other stuff," Daniel added, pointing out the handful of men he'd observed during the presentation.

"I'm familiar with three of them already," Frank admitted. "Good call. Do you want me to see if my lieutenant will bring you in on the investigation? He might be up for it."

"Not yet. Want to stay off the radar, for now."

Frank frowned. "I'm not sure I like you wandering around out there freelancing. This is my case, and I don't want it messed up by someone who's not working on the same page as me."

"I'll be careful."

Carter didn't seem appeased by Daniel's assurance, but one of the meeting attendees interrupted at that point, pulling Frank away. Daniel took advantage of the opportunity to look for Rose again. He spotted her, finally, sitting alone near the front of the room, her hands clasped tightly in her lap.

She gave a start when he dropped into the chair next to her. Her silvery-brown eyes met his, wide and troubled.

"Not hungry?"

She shook her head.

"Did you come here with Melissa?"

"No, I got a ride with a neighbor." She looked toward an older woman standing in line at the refreshment table. "She wanted to stay around a little bit, see if she could get a word with Detective Carter."

"I could drive you home." He hadn't known he'd make the offer until the words spilled from his lips. He had planned to hang around the place a little longer, watch the crowd in case he'd missed something.

"Not necessary," she said softly. "Besides, aren't you looking for the killer? You don't want to sneak out too early and miss him."

So she *did* know who he was. He'd begun to suspect as much. "Don't mind if I sit here while I look, do you?"

Her lips curved slightly. "Free country."

He settled next to her, his arm brushing hers. Sparks flew, sizzling along his nerve endings. He hadn't felt anything quite like her effect on him in a long time.

Too long.

"So why didn't you just tell me who you were the first time we met?" Rose asked.

"Wanted to keep a low profile."

"Until it came time to trick Melissa into giving you my name and address."

"Technically, I already knew your address."

The look she gave him singed his eyebrows. "So, I'm guessing that you're not really in the market for a wedding planner, either."

"No." He changed the subject. "Earlier tonight, you looked back in the crowd and saw someone or something that upset you. What was it?"

"I just got a creepy feeling," she answered tightly, looking away. He knew immediately it wasn't the truth. Not the full truth, anyway. But she showed no signs of budging from her vague explanation, so he tabled the discussion for later.

"He was here, wasn't he?" she added, half whispering.

He didn't have to ask whom she was talking about. "I can't see him not showing up for something like this."

Her pale face went a shade whiter. "I could feel him."

He frowned. "Feel him?"

Her gaze darted up to meet his. "I know that sounds crazy."

Not entirely. He'd felt Orion in the room tonight, too. But his hunch was based less on emotion or some intangible sensibility than a scientist's certainty that, given all the variables at play, it was nearly impossible for a killer like Orion to resist the opportunity to see the fruits of his labors.

He knew Orion had been here because the killer was incapable of staying away.

"Detective Carter gave a good presentation." Rose changed the subject abruptly. "I've overheard a lot of women saying that they feel safer just knowing he's on the case."

"How about you?" Daniel asked. "Do you feel safer?"

She cocked her head. "I don't know. I'm glad he agreed to speak, though. Women in this neighborhood need to know how to even the playing field between them and the killer."

Daniel didn't think a single talk from a cop was enough to make the women of Southside any safer, but he understood Rose's need to do something constructive to make sense of the loss she'd experienced. "There are more things that can be done. Self-defense courses—"

"I'm giving that serious thought."

"I know a guy who runs a dojo near here." Daniel had made it to black belt under the tutelage of Tommy Kim; the guy was great at what he did and he was particularly good at teaching women how to not only protect themselves but to increase their awareness of their surroundings. "I'll see if he's interested in doing a basic self-protection course for women."

The hint of a smile faded from Rose's face. "I wonder if any of this will make any difference."

"Can't hurt," Daniel pointed out. "If a little more awareness and a few well-aimed kicks saves a woman, then we're ahead of where we are today. And then maybe we'll have a description of Orion."

"You and Detective Carter seem to know each other. Have you met before? Before you came to town, I mean."

Daniel nodded, not sure how much he was willing to share about his past with Rose. "I grew up around this neighborhood. Dated his sister in college. He was just a teenager then."

"You're from Birmingham, then?"

"Born and raised. How about you?"

"I just moved here a few months ago. I grew up east of here in a little dot on the map called Willow Grove."

He'd heard of it, but he'd never been there. "What brought you to Birmingham?"

"Business. There just wasn't enough of it in Willow Grove." Rose's voice was light enough, but he saw a flicker of sadness in her eyes that suggested her decision to relocate wasn't quite as simple as her brief explanation implied.

There was little about Rose Browning that was simple.

"Sure I can't give you a ride home? Your neighbor doesn't seem inclined to leave anytime soon."

"I'll catch a ride with Melissa if I can find her."

"I'm pretty sure she left just a few minutes ago."

Rose's brow furrowed. "Damn."

"No trouble to drive you home," he assured her.

She cocked her head slightly, her pale brown eyes narrowing as she looked at him with a hint of curiosity. "Do you consider me a suspect or something?"

Not a suspect, exactly. But she knew something she wasn't telling. "Maybe I just like you."

She made a soft sound that might have been a huff of laughter. "I don't think that's it."

"Well, I do like you," he said firmly, surprised to find that it was the truth.

"You think I know something about your killer."

"Do you?" he countered.

"Only what I hear in the news or read in the paper."

Once again, he was certain there was something she wasn't telling him. But Rose had already proved to be very good at keeping her own counsel.

Maybe she just needed an incentive to spill what she knew. "If you'll let me take you home, maybe I'll tell you a few things you don't know about the killer."

Curiosity flitted across her composed face. She pushed to her feet. "Okay, I'll tell my neighbor I'm leaving."

Daniel watched her go, his gaze lingering on the curve of her hips swaying gracefully as she crossed to speak to her friend. Yeah, he liked her, all right.

Maybe a little too much.

Chapter Five

The veils had disappeared, Rose reminded herself, tamping down the dread that had weighted her down for most of the evening. Once Frank Carter had started talking, the veils had begun to fade from the faces of the people around her. By the time she and Daniel left the library, she hadn't seen any death veils at all.

What did that mean? That he'd decided against killing again so soon? Or that he'd chosen a victim; one she hadn't seen as she was leaving the meeting?

"Warm enough?" Daniel fiddled with the car heater.

"I'm fine," she lied. She wasn't fine. She felt shaky and out of control, as if she were skating along the edge of an endless abyss every second she spent with Daniel.

She was attracted to him. Hard to deny it, given the way her arm still tingled where he'd held it as he'd helped her into the passenger seat of his Jeep or the way her heart was pounding like a drum line in her chest. Just the thought of his storm-cloud eyes watching her was enough to make her shiver.

But there were a lot of attractive men in the world. Hormones alone dictated that she'd find some of them tempting. She'd spent a lot of years ignoring those temptations, armed with the certainty that, when she finally met the right man for her, the evidence would be written all over his face and hers.

God, what she'd give to have those true-love veils back.

She felt as if she were flying blind, helpless to know whether the man who made her toes tingle and her breath catch in her chest was going to make her the happiest woman on earth or shatter her heart into a thousand bleeding pieces.

She'd had no idea just how much she'd depended on the true-love veils until she'd lost them.

Daniel pulled the Jeep up the steep drive at the front of her house and cut the engine. He gazed forward through the windshield at her garage door, his profile limned with golden light from the streetlamps. "Want me to come in and take a look around to make sure the place is secure?"

Pride urged her to tell him she'd be fine, but good sense won out. No point in taking stupid risks. If Daniel Hartman wanted to make sure she was alone, safely locked behind sturdy dead bolts, she'd be foolish to refuse the offer. "Sure. I'd appreciate that."

At the front door, he held out his hand for her keys. She passed them over, her fingers brushing his. A now familiar jolt of energy darted up her arm.

He unlocked the dead bolt and opened the door, keeping her behind him until he'd turned on the lights, setting the foyer awash with warm gold light from the overhead chandelier. He locked the door behind them and moved from the narrow foyer into the living room, turning on the lamps and giving the room a thorough walk-through.

They moved from room to room, repeating the ritual, then climbed the polished stairs to the second floor and started the process all·over again. They ended their tour in the bedroom at the end of the hall, the one Rose had chosen for herself because of the tall windows offering a stunning view of the Birmingham city skyline.

Daniel paused in front of the windows, moving aside the curtain panels to get a better look at the view. On impulse, Rose reached for the light switch, plunging them into darkness alleviated only by the city lights. Daniel turned his head, his profile visible only in silhouette.

"The view's easier to see with the lights off," she said.

"I'd forgotten what a pretty sight Birmingham can be at night," Daniel murmured as she joined him by the window.

"I love it on a rainy night, when the water fractures all the lights into a thousand little diamonds." Without planning to, Rose moved close enough to Daniel that his arm brushed hers. She breathed deeply, taking in his clean, masculine scent, the tug of attraction setting her nerve endings on fire.

He turned toward her, his head dipping closer. "Why did you really turn off the lights?"

She took a shaky breath, her heart hammering. Why *had* she turned off the lights? To set up a moment like this? To feel his hand on her face, his breath stir her hair? "Why did you really want to come in?" she responded, her voice raspy and low. She wished she could see the expression in his eyes.

She wasn't sure who moved first, but before she could take another breath, his lips were touching hers. The kiss radiated warmth through her, igniting a slow burn that started deep in her belly and began to spread. The kiss grew fiercer, more demanding, pouring kerosene on the flames licking at her belly and down to her core.

Rising on tiptoe, she wrapped her arms around his neck and pulled him closer, urging him to fan the fire he'd started inside her. His tongue brushed her mouth, demanding entry, and she could do nothing but part her lips and let him inside.

He tasted like coffee and sweet cream, dark and rich with a bittersweet edge. He enclosed her in his arms, pulled her flush against him, until she felt every angle and plane of his lean, muscular body. She parted her thighs, welcomed the hard heat of his pelvis against hers, wondering at the little sparks shooting through her body from her hips to her breasts.

When he suddenly set her away from him, her body buzzed with shock. "What—"

"This can't happen." His raw voice sent another shiver down her spine. "Not a good idea."

She stepped back on wobbly legs, sinking to the edge of the bed when the backs of her knees hit the mattress. Embarrassment washed over her, burning her cheeks. "I'm sorry."

He moved away and turned on the light. Rose squinted against the sudden illumination, the glow from the fixture over the bed overwhelming her dilated pupils. It took a second for her eyes to adjust enough to see him standing in her doorway, his gaze wary. Silence stretched between them, unbearable.

"Lock the front door behind me," he said, snapping the band of tension. He headed for the staircase without giving her a chance to respond.

She caught up with him at the landing, forcing herself not to reach out and touch him, pulling him back with her to the bedroom. How humiliating would that be?

Her sudden craving for closeness, for the feel of someone else's skin against hers, knocked her off balance. Was she reacting to the fear, the knowledge that, somewhere out there, hidden by the shelter of night, a killer stalked the streets around her, looking for his next prey? Was she reaching out for warmth, for a connection to someone else, someone who could protect her from the monster in the night?

She'd always been resolute in her determination to wait for her one true love. But losing that certainty had left her vulnerable to the unpredictable world around her, at the mercy of her own frantic fears and needs.

Vulnerable enough to make a fool of herself in front of a virtual stranger.

Daniel turned at the door, gazing at her with storm-dark eyes. "Lock the dead bolt and the knob lock," he said.

She nodded, rubbing her damp palms against her skirt.

He hesitated before reaching for the doorknob, his head cocking slightly to one side as if he was thinking about saying something else. But he must have thought better of it, for he turned quickly and opened the door, slipping out into the night without saying another word.

Rose engaged the dead bolt and the lock on the

doorknob, shutting off the foyer lights so that Daniel wouldn't see her watching him as he exited her driveway and drove back toward Dunbar.

ROSE'S CELL PHONE rang Wednesday morning as she was walking outside to check her mailbox. "Browning Wedding Services."

"I thought the meeting last night was great. Didn't you?" Melissa said without preamble, her voice tinny and faraway through the cell phone.

Rose tucked the phone between her chin and shoulder, opening the mailbox. "I think it went well," she answered, heat rising in her cheeks as she remembered how her night had gone after the meeting.

"Listen, I've changed my appointment at Bella to this afternoon instead of tomorrow. Mark's taking me out for our three-year dating anniversary tomorrow night, so I'm taking the afternoon off to make myself gorgeous for it. I'm supposed to be at Bella this afternoon at two o'clock—she has several veils she wants me to see. Can you make it?"

"Yeah, sure. I can be there." Not that she'd have much to do; Melissa always had a pretty good idea of exactly what she wanted, which meant there was little for Rose to do but sit back and let her client haggle with the dress-shop owner.

"Great! Listen, I've got to run. See you at two." Melissa rang off.

Rose shut off the phone and flipped through the mail on her way back inside. She paused, puzzled, at finding a small, white envelope with nothing on it. No address, no stamp—nothing.

Weird.

Frowning, she took a letter opener from the utility drawer in the kitchen and slit open the envelope. Inside she found a small card embossed on edges with silver butterflies. Plain, block letters in black ink sprawled across the center of the card. "Thanks for setting up the meeting. It was a big help."

There was no signature on the note, nothing but those two brief sentences in black ink on the white card.

Rose dropped the card on the counter, her hands trembling. Why hadn't the sender signed the card? Why was there no return address on the envelope?

She closed her eyes, trying to calm the sudden jangle of her nerves. It was just a thank-you note, probably sent by someone too shy to sign her name. Except the writing didn't look feminine, at all. The bold, black letters seemed masculine. Forceful. Threatening.

A picture of the note flashed through her mind, stained with crimson slashes. She opened her eyes quickly, her pulse ratcheting up to a gallop.

It was a threat. A sneer from a killer who wanted her to know there was nothing she could do to stop him.

Heart pounding, she reached for the phone.

THE BIRMINGHAM Motor Lodge didn't offer much in the way of amenities, but incongruently, it had free wireless Internet connection, and Daniel took full advantage of it Wednesday morning.

Anything to get his mind off kissing Rose Browning.

Unfortunately, Rose was the focus of his Internet search. She obviously had no intention of spilling her secrets to him, not even after a mind-blowing kiss, and he hadn't quite sunk to the level of using seduction as an interrogation tool.

But he needed to know more about her. Because she knew something about Orion, something she wasn't telling. Maybe something she didn't even realize.

If she had some sort of connection with the killer, Daniel needed to know about it.

He started with something she'd told him last night. Before the kiss. She'd moved to Birmingham only a few months earlier from the town where she'd grown up.

The town of Willow Grove.

The official Web site for Willow Grove didn't amount to much, and there was nothing on the Web page to indicate that Rose Browning had ever had much standing in the community. However, the site listed contact information for the mayor, Floyd Chamberlain. If Daniel was lucky, Mr. Chamberlain would have heard of him. If he was very lucky, the mayor would be the talkative sort.

It took a little flirting with the mayor's female aide to get through to the mayor himself, but eventually Floyd Chamberlain took Daniel's call. "Dr. Hartman, it's a pleasure to talk to you. I saw you last year on a Fox News segment on school shootings. Our school system has implemented several of your suggestions."

"Hope they've worked for you."

The mayor's booming voice rumbled over the phone line. "Oh, they have, Dr. Hartman! They have! We don't have much in the way of crime around here, but teachers at the high school say the warning signs you mentioned helped them stop problems before they happened. What can I do for you today, sir?"

Daniel decided the truth, or a close approximation, was the way to go. "I'm doing a case study of some murders in Birmingham, and I've come across someone from your town. Rose Browning. Are you familiar with her?"

There was the briefest of pauses before the mayor said, "Certainly am. Very sweet, lovely girl. I was sorry to see her move away to the big city."

Chamberlain was saying all the right things, but that brief hesitation, along with a guarded tone in his voice, piqued Daniel's interest. "She's peripherally involved in the cases I'm looking into—recently lost a friend in a violent crime."

"Oh, no. Poor thing." The mayor sounded genuinely distressed. "I'd hoped once in a lifetime was enough."

"It's happened to her before?" Daniel opened his notepad and scrabbled through the motel desk drawers for a pen.

"Last December." Chamberlain made a soft clicking noise with his tongue. "I reckon you know she's a wedding planner—"

"Yes."

"She'd planned a wedding for Carrie and Dillon Granville. Carrie was a real sweet girl, from a real good family."

"But Dillon wasn't?" Daniel surmised from the tone of the mayor's voice.

"Oh, he was a good-lookin' boy. Lord knows, half the girls in town were crazy over him, but he could be wild as a hare when he got to drinkin'. And he got to drinkin' a lot." The mayor's voice tightened. "Carrie's mama and daddy didn't want her to marry Dillon. He didn't have a real steady job and he had that wild streak, but Carrie was convinced he was the man for her, and so was Rose. She helped Carrie make up her mind."

Daniel frowned. That didn't sound like the Rose he knew.

Then again, how much did he know about her? The first time he'd seen her, she'd been sitting alone in a bar, looking like bait for the next horn dog who walked through the door.

Maybe she had a wild side he didn't know about.

"Rose planned the wedding for Carrie and Dillon, free of charge, since Dillon didn't have much money and Carrie's mama and daddy refused to be part of the whole thing."

"I take it things ended badly."

"Last December, apparently, Carrie had decided she'd taken enough of Dillon's craziness and set about leaving him. Dillon wouldn't let her go, so he shot her dead. Rose had decided to visit them that day, take them a Christmas present." Chamberlain lowered his voice. "Poor Rose got there just in time to see Dillon kill himself."

Daniel's stomach clenched in sympathy. "My God."

"She took it real bad, of course. Wasn't that long before she moved away. And now you say it happened to her again?"

"She didn't witness it this time," Daniel said.

"Thank goodness for that, at least."

"Thank you, Mr. Chamberlain, for your time. Appreciate it," Daniel said, meaning it.

"I don't know what I've done but prattle on like an old fool," Chamberlain responded, but he couldn't hide the pleasure in his voice. "I hope you don't think Rose had anything to do with the crimes you're investigating—"

"Not at all," Daniel assured him. He didn't think, for a moment, that Rose Browning had anything to do with the murders.

He was less sure, however, that she had no knowledge about the killer that she hadn't yet chosen to share with him.

But what kind of secret could she be keeping?

His cell phone rang as he was heading out the door to find some lunch. Shrugging on his coat, he answered. "Hartman."

"Daniel, it's Rose Browning."

The warm timbre of her voice sent a shudder of heat rushing through him. "How'd you get my cell-phone number?"

"Melissa gave it to me." She hesitated. "Something's happened. I don't know what it means."

He went instantly tense. "You okay?"

"Yes, but—could you come here as soon as possible? I need to show you something."

"I'll be right there." Ringing off, he locked the motel-room door behind him and raced for the parking lot.

"Do you think it means anything?" Rose gazed up at Daniel, hoping he'd tell her she was letting her imagination run away with her. But the grim set of his mouth squelched that hope.

"Don't suppose you were wearing gloves when you opened it?"

"No, sorry. I didn't think to—"

"No reason you should." Daniel put his hand on her shoulder, sparking a wildfire down her arm before his hand fell away. "I'd like to have this fingerprinted and analyzed, anyway. Mind being fingerprinted so we can eliminate your prints?"

"Of course not. I'll do whatever you want." She caught her lower lip between her teeth, afraid to ask the next obvious question. She forced herself to voice it, anyway. "Do you think it's from him?"

Daniel met her worried gaze, his expression calm, but serious. "I don't know. From what I know of Orion, he hasn't ever tried to contact anyone—the press or police or any future victims—"

"You think I might be a future victim?"

"I'm not saying that."

"But it's possible."

"Any woman in the world is potentially his victim." Daniel caught her hand in his. "I don't think you should panic until we know a little more about the note, though. Could be from someone in the neighborhood who simply forgot to sign it."

She could tell he didn't really believe that, but he was right about one thing. The last thing she needed to do was to panic. The sadistic bastard who was killing the women of Southside fed on panic and fear. The only way to beat him was to keep her head and stay alert.

She took a bracing breath. "Okay. What do I do next?"

"Come with me to the South precinct to get printed. Have a plastic bag I could use to protect this?" He gestured toward the card on the counter.

Rose retrieved a plastic sandwich bag from the pantry and took it to Daniel. He used a pair of tweezers to maneuver the note and its envelope into the bag, then tucked the bag in his pocket. "Let's go."

Daniel led her outside to his Jeep, his hand warm against the small of her back. He handed her into the passenger seat, his fingers lingering on hers for a moment. "This could be a break, Rose. Could be the break we need."

Or it could be the beginning of a killer's campaign of terror, Rose thought.

With her as his next target.

Chapter Six

"We found one set of prints on the note," Frank told Daniel, his gaze drifting across the room to where Rose sat in a chair by the wall. "Hers."

Daniel had feared as much. "And the handwriting?"

"We've got our analysts on it, but that could take a while." Frank glanced at Rose again. "How's she holding up?"

"She's scared, but holding it together."

"Wonder why she called you instead of me?" A faint undertone of suspicion threaded through Frank's voice.

"I think she was afraid she was overreacting. Easier to pass it by me than someone official."

"How long have you two known each other?"

"A few days. I met her through her friend Melissa."

"Melissa Bannerman? How do you know her?"

Daniel nodded. "She's a publisher. I write books."

Frank looked suspicious, but he dropped the subject. "Maybe that note will be the break we need."

Daniel wasn't so sure. Without fingerprints, all they had was the handwriting. Great, if they found a suspect and could connect him to the block printing, but useless until then. "You through with Ms. Browning?"

"Not much more she can add at the moment. I'm going to canvass her neighbors, see if anyone saw anything." Frank grabbed his jacket and headed for the exit.

Daniel crossed to where Rose sat, tense and wide-eyed, by the wall. "Done here. Think you can handle a little lunch?"

"I don't know. I'm feeling a little queasy."

"Nerves." He led her to the door. "We'll grab something light and see how it goes. What are you in the mood for?"

She flashed him a lopsided grin. "Pepto-Bismol."

He chuckled. "How about a BLT on wheat? I know a place just around the corner."

"I'm not sure I'm up for a lunch crowd."

"We'll grab something to go."

The diner Daniel had in mind was a hole in the wall tucked between a dry cleaner's and a stationery store in Forest Park. He parked the Jeep and cut the engine. "I was half afraid this place wouldn't still be here," he admitted. "Haven't been back in a while. Lots of things have changed."

A blast of fragrant warmth and the murmur of a lunch crowd greeted them inside the diner. Rose decided on a chicken salad with tomato, while Daniel chose a BLT and coleslaw. Within minutes, they were back in the car, heading to Rose's.

Rose said. "Was this diner here when you were younger?"

"Yeah, though it was more of a mom-and-pop place then. Not as trendy." The place had passed on to the second generation, a brother and sister with a much more bohemian sense of style and cuisine than their meat-and-three parents. But the food was still good and affordable and the service had seemed quick and friendly. "Do you eat out or in more often?"

"In," she said with a half smile. "Cheaper that way."

"Hard to start a business in a new town. You buying your house or renting?"

"Buying. I loved it the moment I saw it." Her eyes softened as if she were reliving the first time she'd seen the house. "It had been renovated a couple of years ago, as a rental, but the owner was tired of dealing with transient and student renters, so he jumped on my first offer to buy it."

"Putting down roots, huh?"

She nodded. "It was time."

"Nothing left for you in Willow Grove?"

Her gaze lifted, a hint of wariness in her eyes. "I have family there, but as far as business…"

"Parents? Brothers and sisters?"

"Two sisters. My sister, Lily, lives with her husband in Borland. Only Iris is still in Willow Grove."

Daniel pulled into Rose's driveway, parking behind her Impala. "Nice that they're both close."

Her expression shuttered. "Yeah."

Interesting, Daniel thought. Her reticence about her sisters suggested there was more to the story. Were she and her sisters estranged?

He followed her into the kitchen and laid their food out on the table while Rose poured them two glasses of iced tea. She handed him a glass and sat at the kitchen table. He slid in across from her.

Rose tried a bite of her sandwich, making a low,

humming sound of pleasure that sent blood racing south of his belt. "This is amazing," she commented after washing down her first bite with a sip of tea. "It's got pecans in it, and grapes—"

"Guess you were hungry, after all?" he murmured.

She took another bite, making that same moaning sound that sent a shudder of need skating down his spine.

He took a deep breath and forced his mind back to the reason he was here in the first place. "Maybe you should see if one of your sisters could come stay with you for a while. Until we know more about the note you received."

She looked at him through narrowed eyes. "You think I'm in danger living here alone?"

"I'd feel better if you weren't living alone. That's all."

She put down her sandwich. "I can't ask my sisters to drop their lives and come babysit me."

"Maybe they wouldn't mind."

"I'm a big girl. I'll keep my eyes open and take those self-defense classes we talked about. Maybe get an alarm installed. I'll be fine." She managed a smile that he didn't quite buy.

He couldn't remember seeing a genuine smile from her, he realized. The Granville murder-suicide must've done a real number on her.

"You think last night's meeting did any good?" Rose asked.

"Don't think it did any harm."

There was an odd quality to her silence that caught his gaze. A frown creased her forehead and her lower lip was pinched between her teeth.

"You disagree?" Daniel asked.

She looked at him. "It's too early to know, isn't it?"

He cocked his head. "It's because you think the killer was there last night, isn't it?"

"You thought so, too."

He nodded. "But maybe it's a good thing he saw his victims aren't going to lie down and take it from him in the future."

"Or maybe he saw the crowd as a big buffet table full of goodies to sample," she muttered.

"I don't think it hurts that those women now know a little more about how to protect themselves from him. Safety in numbers, locking doors—"

"All the things people are supposed to remember but never do," Rose murmured.

"Or refuse to do," Daniel countered. "Like have a family member—say, a sister—come stay with them."

She darted a look at him. "Touché."

He gathered up the remains of their lunch and dumped it in the trash bin. "What are your plans for the rest of the day?"

"I have to meet Melissa later to help her pick out a veil for her wedding dress." Rose hooked her arm over the back of her chair and shot him a bemused look. "What are you going to do if she pursues that book deal you snookered her with?"

He shrugged and walked back to the table, close enough that she had to lean her head back to look him in the eye. "Maybe I'll take her up on it. I wouldn't have used it as an excuse if it wasn't a possibility."

"What about telling her you might need a wedding planner?"

"Not in the market at the moment."

"Been there, done that?"

A sliver of old guilt embedded itself in his gut. "Almost been there, almost done that."

Her eyes narrowed, as if his response intrigued her. But to his relief she didn't pursue the topic, asking instead, "Does your friend, Frank, know you're looking into these murders?"

"Does now," Daniel admitted. "Probably going to have to go official now, see if I can talk someone at the Birmingham P.D. into letting me in on the case."

"You don't like going through channels?"

He met her curious gaze. "They can be inhibiting."

She cocked her head to one side, her eyes narrowing. "You were hunting for him that night in the bar, weren't you?"

He sat across the table from her. "So were you."

She looked down at her clasped hands and didn't reply.

"Weren't you?" he prodded.

"I just wanted to get out and mingle."

He shook his head. "But you weren't mingling. You were watching. You were looking for Orion."

Her eyebrows lifted. "Orion?"

"That's what I call him."

"The hunter?" She gave him a look. "A bit cliché."

He shrugged, a little annoyed. What did she know about serial killers? "It fits."

"How many are there?" Rose asked.

He cut his eyes at her. "Murders?"

"You said he didn't start here in Birmingham. How many other women has he killed?"

He shook his head. "I'm not sure."

"Ballpark figure."

He sighed. "At least twenty connected by signature and modus operandi. I'm pretty sure there are more."

"Twenty?" She looked ill.

"That I know of."

Her expression darkened. "How do you do it?"

"Do what?"

"Immerse yourself in so much violence and death." She turned her face away from him, her profile distant. "I mean, you seek it out, don't you? To write about it?"

"To prevent it," he said softly. "I want to find Orion and stop him before he kills anyone else."

She didn't respond right away, giving him time to wonder why he had opened up to her like that. He tended to keep his own counsel about the cases he studied and especially about his own motivations. He tried to be clinical and objective, to see the crimes as puzzles to be solved rather than real lives shattered and destroyed. But at its core, what he did was about stopping very bad men from doing more evil.

Men like Orion.

That's why he was here—wasn't it?—when every instinct he had was screaming at him that Rose Browning was dangerous to him on a lot of different levels. No matter how attractive he found her, no matter how much he wanted to scoop her up out of her chair, take her up to her bedroom and finish what they'd started the night before, he couldn't shake the feeling that Rose knew more about Orion than she was admitting.

"I can't stop wondering why you were at Alice's

apartment that morning." He leaned toward her. "Melissa said you met Alice only the night before. Why would you go to her apartment the next morning?"

Her expression shuttered. "I told you, I called her workplace and she wasn't there."

"And you just offered to go to a virtual stranger's apartment to check on her?" Daniel shook his head, conviction tightening his gut. "You already knew something had happened to her, didn't you?"

"Her employee seemed upset on the phone. It wasn't far to Alice's apartment, so I went to check."

"Very altruistic."

"What exactly are you implying?"

"You were hunting Orion in the bar. Looking for him at the other bar, where you met Alice. What do you know about him?"

Her eyelids flickered, but she didn't respond. He stood, rounding the table to her side. She looked up at him, fear and something else in her eyes.

Something that looked a lot like guilt.

Daniel's stomach knotted. "Who is he, Rose?"

"I don't know."

He clenched his fists and crowded her, his voice hardening. "I don't believe you."

The stricken look on her face caught him off guard. He stepped back, bumping into the chair. It banged to the floor, making Rose flinch.

Daniel picked the chair up, surprised to find his hands shaking. He wasn't prone to anger, especially not while interviewing suspects. He was the master of control. The one who manipulated situations and events, not the other way around.

Yet, here he was, on the verge of putting his fist through the nearest wall.

He needed to get out of here. Get some air. Some perspective. "I have to go."

She nodded, her eyes shiny with unshed tears. "Yeah."

She walked with him as far as the living room and stopped, letting him cross to the front door alone. He opened the door and turned to look at her. She stood with arms folded across her stomach, her gaze unreadable.

"I'll be back," he said.

"I know." Her soft reply had a plaintive edge that softened his anger.

Back in his Jeep, Daniel closed his eyes and laid his head back on the headrest. But he couldn't get Rose's tear-bright eyes out of his mind.

Or the look of guilt on her face when he'd told her he didn't believe her.

He'd practically accused her of knowing who Orion was—yet if she knew, why had she been bar-crawling in search of him? And if she knew who the killer was and how he operated, why would she have gone to Alice Donovan's house looking for her? Orion never killed his victims at home and he never dumped them where they lived.

So she didn't know Orion. But she knew something.

What was she hiding?

ROSE ARRIVED at Bella a little after two, still reeling from her confrontation with Daniel. He didn't trust her, and who could blame him? She *was* keeping secrets.

Bella Charmaigne met her at the door with a long-suffering smile. "Ms. Bannerman's already here. She brought her gown so that she could see how the veils looked with it." She motioned for Rose to take a seat outside the dressing area.

A moment later Melissa emerged from the dressing room on a cloud of snowy silk and lace. Rose lifted her gaze to Melissa's smiling face. Her heart plummeted.

Shimmery gashes wept crimson over Melissa's face.

Rose swallowed convulsively, fighting for control.

Melissa modeled the gauzy drape, turning to look at herself from all angles in the bank of full-length mirrors. "It matches my dress perfectly." She lifted the long silk skirt of the wedding gown and waved it gently, admiring the glossy ripple of fabric. Rose looked down at her hands, noting the pasty whiteness of her tightly clenched knuckles.

I have to tell her, she thought.

"Well?" There was an edginess to Melissa's voice, an imperious tone that caught Rose off guard. Rose forced herself to look up.

"Do you like the veil or not?" Melissa's choice of words popped a big bubble of hysteria in Rose's stomach. Adrenaline spilled out, sending wild tremors through her nervous system.

She pushed to her feet. "Melissa, you've got to change and come with me."

Melissa's face crinkled with surprise. "Where?"

"Somewhere private." She wasn't handling the situation well, but she didn't know what to say, how to explain. All she knew was that she couldn't tell Melissa about the death veil here, in the middle of a dress shop.

Melissa looked perplexed. "It can't wait?"

Rose took a desperate step toward Melissa. "No, it can't. Please get dressed."

Melissa hesitated a moment, as if to protest, but she finally pivoted and returned to the dressing room. Rose glanced at Bella, not surprised to find the dressmaker's expression as wary as Melissa's had been. She looked away and started pacing off her nervous energy until Melissa reemerged from the dressing room wearing a business suit.

She handed the veil she'd selected to Bella. "Put this on my account and hold it for me, okay?"

Bella scurried away to ring up the sale while Melissa draped her garment bag over one arm and grabbed Rose's elbow with the other hand. She led her outside at a brisk, angry pace, stopping when they reached the silver Lexus parked in front of the dress shop. She put the dress in the backseat and faced her, eyes flashing fire. "What the hell's going on?"

Rose's legs trembled with the urge to run far away from the skeptical world, to a place where she'd never have to try to explain the unexplainable again. She pushed her fingers through her hair with shaking hands and took a deep breath. "Okay. When you hired me, you checked my references, right?"

Melissa's eyes narrowed. "Right."

"And people in Willow Grove probably had a good bit to say about me, didn't they?"

Melissa's lips quirked. "They think you're some kind of romance wizard. Said you were quite the matchmaker."

"I used to be. I used to be a lot of things."

Melissa gestured impatiently. "What's going on, Rose?"

"I see—" Rose paused, wondering if there was a better word than *veil*. She could think of nothing. "I see veils."

Melissa blinked. "Veils? Wedding veils?"

Rose shook her head impatiently. "Not wedding veils. Just—veils. Shimmery veils over some people's faces. I used to see good ones. Happy ones." Rose rushed through a quick explanation of the true-love veils.

"So you see true-love veils and use them to match people?" Curiosity battled with skepticism in Melissa's dark blue eyes.

"Yes. Or, at least, I did," Rose admitted. "But this is about something else—"

Melissa's expression darkened. "Something bad?"

Rose looked up at Melissa, willing the girl to believe. Taking another deep breath, she plunged ahead, saying the words she'd never said out loud before, even to herself.

"I see death."

Chapter Seven

"You see death." Melissa's posture, expression, tone of voice all conveyed rejection.

"I know, it sounds crazy—"

"It doesn't sound crazy. It *is* crazy. First you say you can see true-love veils, but, oops, you don't see those anymore because now you see death. Do you even hear what you're saying?" Melissa reached for the car door handle.

Rose caught her arm. "I know it sounds impossible."

Melissa whirled around. "Let go of me."

"You know me. Would I say this if it wasn't true?"

Melissa shook her head, her brow furrowed. "I don't think I know you at all." She turned to open her car door.

"I saw a death veil on Alice Donovan's face," Rose blurted.

Melissa froze.

"That night at the club," Rose continued, "when she was dancing and she turned toward us, I saw it on her face."

Melissa turned slowly, a dangerous glitter in her eyes. "Don't even—"

"That's why I left right after she did. I wanted to catch her before she left, to try to warn her."

Melissa's shoulders stiffened. "Did you?"

Rose nodded. "I told her what I was seeing."

"And she called you crazy."

"More or less," Rose admitted, despair washing over her.

Enunciating her words slowly and carefully, Melissa asked, "Did you do anything to Alice?"

Rose stared at Melissa, hurt. "Of course not. I was trying to warn her."

"Like you're trying to warn me."

The tears burning behind Rose's eyes spilled down her cheeks. "I don't care if you think I'm nuts. Could it hurt to be extra careful over the next few days?"

"You know I had a new alarm system put in my house last week. My car has a state-of-the-art security system. I'll be fine."

"Just remember what I said, okay? Maybe you and Mark should get away for a few days. For your anniversary—make it a long weekend. Give the police time to track this man down."

Melissa's eyebrows rose. "You think the slasher's going to get me? Like he got Alice?"

Rose looked away from the shimmering veil marring Melissa's pretty face. "Maybe not if you get out of town for a few days."

Melissa shook her head. "I have a wedding to plan, and now I have to find a new planner. I'm not going anywhere." She slid behind the wheel of her car and started to close the door.

Rose put her hand on the door, stopping Melissa from closing it. "Don't go anywhere alone, Melissa."

"Get your hand off my car door." Melissa's voice grated.

Rose stepped back. Melissa slammed the door shut, gunned the engine and whipped out of the parking slot, tires whining.

Knuckling the tears from her eyes, Rose trudged to her own car. She felt achy and heart-sore, weighted down by the shroud of despair blanketing every part of her life these days.

Considering her emotional state, it should have come as no surprise when she arrived home to find her sister Iris pacing the back patio. She'd probably sensed Rose's agitation all the way from Willow Grove.

Rose parked her Chevy, peering through the windshield at her sister. Iris glared back, her posture tense.

Lovely.

"What the hell is going on, Rose?" Iris greeted her.

"Nice to see you, too."

Eyes flashing with equal parts concern and irritation, Iris held up a newspaper with a large headline: Police Confirm Link Between Three Murders. "I was reading this story about a serial killer stalking your neighborhood when I came across your name. You helped set up a neighborhood meeting to address the issue? How civic of you."

Rose sighed. "Since when do you get the *Birmingham News?*"

"Since my flighty sister pulled up stakes and headed to Birmingham without any notice."

Rose pressed her lips together. "I'm fine."

"And how did the neighborhood meeting go?"

"It went well. Lots of good information."

To Rose's surprise, Iris's coffee-colored eyes filled with tears and her face crumpled. She sank onto the wrought iron bench by the door. "Rosie, what have I done?"

Rose sat beside her sister, putting her hand on Iris's knee. "Done? Why would you think you've done something?"

Iris dashed away a tear with an angry jab of her thumb. "I don't know, maybe because you moved out of the house on a whim and left me there alone, and now you won't return my calls?"

"I'm sorry." Guilt washed over Rose in a dark wave. "I wasn't avoiding you. I guess I was trying to avoid me."

Iris sniffled. "That doesn't make a damned bit of sense."

Rose chuckled through her tears. "I know."

Iris put her arm around Rose's shoulders. "The true-love veils still haven't come back, huh?"

Rose rested her head on her sister's shoulder, tears spilling down her cheeks. Iris's strong arm reminded her of how much she'd given up by isolating herself from her family. Iris's empathic energy radiated down Rose's arm and into her aching chest, drawing out her pain like a magnet.

Iris took in a swift breath, tightening her hold on Rose. "Rose, my God—what's happened to you?"

Rose withdrew from her sister's embrace before Iris could feel the full brunt of her tortured emotions.

"Everything's gone so wrong, and I don't know how to fix it."

"Maybe I can fix it." Iris reached for Rose again, but Rose dodged her touch, not wanting to inflict more pain on her sister. Iris dropped her hand to her lap but held Rose's gaze. "Tell me, Rosie. I promise it'll be better if you share it."

Rose haltingly explained about the death veils, from the first appearance on Dillon Granville's face to her recent experiences. Iris's gaze revealed equal parts compassion and horror, tears sliding over her cheeks and reddening her eyes.

When Rose subsided into soft sniffles, Iris straightened her back. "Okay. You have a different gift now, that's all."

"A terrible gift," Rose muttered. "I don't want it."

Iris brushed Rose's hair away from her face. "I don't blame you, but it is what it is."

"I hate that phrase."

"You were spoiled, you know. Having such a happy gift."

Rose nodded, wiping her eyes with the heels of her palms. "I know you and Lily didn't always like your gifts."

"Lily ran away from hers for years." Iris looked down at her hands. "I never ran from mine, but there've been lots of times I've wanted to. Feeling other people's pain isn't fun."

"But you've been able to help a lot of people."

"And maybe you can help people, too," Iris pointed out. "Like with that meeting."

"A lot of good that did." Rose told Iris about seeing

the death veils on the women in the audience. "What if I paraded the killer's next victim right in front of him?"

"You may never know how many women's lives you saved by helping them know how to avoid danger and protect themselves," Iris countered. "Organizing that meeting and informing women what they're up against was the right thing to do."

"That's what Daniel says, too."

"Daniel?"

Rose flushed. "Daniel Hartman."

Iris looked taken aback. "The criminologist?"

Rose quirked one eyebrow. "You've heard of him?"

"Uh, yeah." Iris looked at her as if she were dumb as a stump. "Daniel Hartman, wonderboy profiler."

He would hate that characterization, Rose thought.

"You've met him?" Iris asked, her voice tinged with awe.

The heat rising up Rose's neck intensified. She'd done a bit more than just meet him, much to her embarrassment. "Yeah."

"Is he as cute in person as he is on TV?"

"I guess." Rose tried to sound noncommittal.

Iris's eyes narrowed. "Just how well *do* you know him?"

"We've met a few times."

"Met."

"Stop it, Iris." She couldn't deny that she found Daniel attractive. But his rebuff after she'd kissed him left her with little indication he returned her feelings. She'd tried to convince herself that he'd kissed her back, that maybe the glitter she'd seen in his eyes had been desire. But the sad fact was, for all her expertise in bringing couples together, her own experiences with romance were limited. She'd been waiting for the true-love veils to tell her when she'd met the man who would own her heart.

What came easily to other women was a puzzle to her.

"Rosie, do you have feelings for him?" Iris asked.

"I can't see the true-love veils anymore," Rose blurted.

Iris's dark eyes narrowed. "Not what I asked."

"How can I know any man is my one true love?"

Iris's lips tightened into a thin line. "What makes you think you ever could?"

Rose glared at her sister. "What's that supposed to mean?"

Iris held her gaze, her expression serious. "Dillon and Carrie Granville were true loves. Soul mates. And he ended up killing her and himself because she was going to leave him."

Rose bit her lip. "I must have made a mistake—"

"What if you didn't?" Iris asked. "What if you saw exactly what you always see? What if they *were* soul mates? True loves? What if all that was true, but they still weren't supposed to be together because Dillon wasn't stable enough to handle it?"

Rose shook her head. "That's not how it works."

Iris laughed, though there was little humor in the sound. "We don't know *how* our gifts work. Lily doesn't really know how her visions work. I don't know why I feel other people's pain when I touch them, and why sometimes it's stronger than other times. And maybe all you ever knew about true-love veils was that they were signposts, pointing to people with the capacity for a forever kind of love. A signpost, not a guarantee."

Rose shook her head again, her sister's words clanging like chaos in her head. That's not the way things were. It couldn't be. From childhood, she'd known with utter certainty that the true-love veils were signs that two people were destined for lifetime happiness with each other. And she'd never been wrong, not in all the years she'd been seeing them.

Not until Carrie and Dillon Granville.

"I kept you from doing something stupid with Paul Abernathy," she reminded Iris. "I saw the true-love veil of Ann Curtis on his face, and I saved you a heartache. And I was right about Lily and McBride, too—"

"There's a difference between probabilities and certainties," Iris said. "The true-love veils told you about probabilities—these two people have what it takes to be happy together if they play their cards right. But it can't promise a good outcome. That's up to the people involved, isn't it?"

Rose pressed her face in her hands. "Then, what was the point of even having that gift, if it was only a maybe?"

Iris touched Rose's cheek. "I guess, that's what you have to find out now that it's gone."

Rose stood, pulled her keys from her pocket and let them in the back door. She led her sister into the living room, crossing to the mirror above the fireplace mantel. She gazed at her haunted reflection and asked the question she dreaded most. "Why do you think I'm seeing death veils now?"

Iris crossed to stand just behind her. Their eyes met in the mirror. "Maybe you're meant to stop the murders."

Rose closed her eyes. "How?"

"I wish I could tell you." Iris put her hands on Rose's

shoulders, the touch electric. Tension flowed out of Rose's arms, pouring through the connection between them. Rose opened her eyes and saw the hollows that seemed to form, like dreadful magic, under her sister's dark eyes.

Rose pulled away from Iris's touch, turning to face her. "You can't heal this. You'll hurt yourself trying."

"I wish I could take it all away from you."

Rose caught Iris's hand in hers, enfolding it between her palms. "Just being here helped. I didn't know just how much I needed to tell you about this."

Iris's smile was pained. "A lot's changed with you. I wish I'd known before now. I wish you'd told Lily or me something so we could have helped you out."

"I know. I'm sorry."

"You want me to tell Lily so she'll know what's going on?"

Rose shook her head. "I'll tell her. I'm a big girl."

Iris tugged Rose's hair. "I brought a bag, just in case. I can stay here tonight. We could do each other's hair and watch cheesy movies." Her eyes took on a teasing glint. "That is, unless you've got a date with the wonderboy profiler."

Relief bubbled up in Rose's throat; her self-imposed estrangement from her sisters had hurt more than she realized. Why had she thought keeping secrets from them would make her life easier? "No date," she assured her sister. "But I have a whole tin of chocolate."

Iris laughed. "I'll go get my bag!"

"HOW MANY of the death veils have you seen?" Iris asked Rose over breakfast Thursday morning.

Rose washed down her bite of bagel with milk. "Twelve."

Iris cocked her head. "Exactly twelve?"

Rose put down the rest of her bagel, her appetite gone. "It's not something I could forget."

Iris reached across the table and squeezed Rose's hand. "I'm sorry, I know this isn't a topic you want to talk about, especially over breakfast, but—"

"But I've been running away from it long enough," Rose finished for her. "I know. You're right."

"Do you remember who those twelve were, how they died—"

"Only eleven are dead, but I can even tell you the dates they died." Those faces, those names were etched in Rose's memory.

"Melissa's the twelfth?"

Rose nodded, the memory of Melissa Bannerman's death veil making her stomach roll.

"Okay. So tell me who the others were." Iris crossed to the refrigerator and removed a magnetized notepad with attached pen that hung on the door. She sat across from Rose. "I know about Dillon. Who's next?"

Pushing aside her revulsion, Rose answered, "Jenny Maitland. She died in a car accident on New Year's Eve. Drunk driver hit her. I saw her earlier in the day, at the grocery store. I tried to tell her to be careful, but she looked at me like I was crazy."

"Nothing new for us Browning girls, right?" Iris smiled, but her eyes were full of empathy as she jotted down a few notes on the notepad. "Who else?"

As Rose named the others, a pattern began to appear. "All foul play of some sort," Iris pointed out.

She was right. Of the twelve death veils Rose had seen over the past ten months, none of the eleven had died of natural causes or simple accidents.

"Violent deaths that might've been prevented." Iris pushed the notepad toward Rose. "Maybe that's why you're seeing them."

"To stop their deaths?" Rose grimaced. "Then, I'm failing miserably."

"Nobody ever said having a special gift would be easy—" A soft trilling sound interrupted Iris. She crossed to the counter where she'd left her purse and answered her cell phone. "Oh, hi, Shelley. What's up?"

Shelley Daniels was a college student who helped Iris at the plant nursery Iris owned. Probably some business question. Rose turned her attention to the list of names.

Eleven people dead. Melissa in grave danger. And apparently Rose was seeing death veils because there was a chance to prevent the deaths.

But how was she supposed to do that?

"And you can't get it going at all?"

Rose looked up at the sound of concern in her sister's voice. Iris's mouth tightened. "No, I know it's a hunk of junk, but it's all I can afford at the moment. I can be there in an hour. I can usually get it running again."

The generator, Rose guessed. Her sister had been fighting with that piece of machinery for four years, ever since she'd started growing tropicals at her nursery.

Iris disconnected and gave Rose an apologetic look. "That was Shelley. The storm that blew through last night knocked out the power at the nursery and she can't get the generator going. I've got to get there within a couple of hours or we're going to lose all the tropicals in the hothouse."

"Go. I'll be fine."

Iris frowned. "Are you sure? Maybe I could call someone to go check on it—"

"You know you're the only one who can ever get that old thing going. Hurry, before the orchids die."

Rose helped Iris pack up her things and walked her to the back door. "Drive carefully, and call me when you get there."

Iris hugged her. "I love you. Thanks for telling me what was bothering you. I promise, you'll figure everything out. You'll know exactly what the veils mean and what you're supposed to do about them. I have faith in you."

Tears pricked Rose's eyes, and she gave her sister a second, fierce hug. "I love you, too. Thanks for everything. You've already made me feel so much better."

Wiping her eyes, she watched her sister drive down the back alley, wishing she could return to Willow Grove with her, back to the life she used to know, the security of a world where the only thing she saw was happiness and hope.

But that world didn't exist, anymore, and Iris was right about one thing: No matter how much she hated the death veils, they obviously weren't going away. The only thing left was to figure out how she was supposed to use them.

And she had to start with Melissa.

"I WAS SURPRISED by your call," Daniel confessed as he entered Melissa Bannerman's office. He'd figured Rose would have already clued her in on his real reason for seeking her out.

Melissa's knowing look as he took the seat across the desk from her gave him little reason to think otherwise. "I wonder why that could be?"

He didn't bother to feign ignorance. "I really am in the market for a publisher for the book we discussed, but you're right, that wasn't my primary reason for coming here."

"You could have just told me that."

"Maybe I should have. Wasn't sure at the time, and I needed information."

"About my relationship with Alice Donovan."

"Someone said you and Alice had plans to go out the night before she died. I wanted to know what you knew."

"What about Rose Browning? You seemed awfully interested in her when I saw you together at the meeting Tuesday night."

He kept his expression neutral, though the memory of Rose Browning's lips, soft and warm beneath his, still lingered. "You mentioned that she was there at the club, as well, and that she'd left soon after Alice."

"You wanted to pump her for information, too?"

"Yes." And he'd wanted to know what she'd been looking for in the bar where he'd seen her earlier, and why she'd fled Alice's apartment when the police had arrived. But he wasn't going to share that information with Melissa.

"There's something you need to know—" Melissa's phone buzzed, stopping her midsentence. Frowning, she picked up the receiver. "Melissa Bannerman." Her frown deepened as she listened to whoever was on the other end. She rose from her chair and walked to the window behind her desk, the phone cord stretching out behind her. "Oh, for God's sake—"

Daniel craned his neck, trying to follow her gaze, but from his seat, he could see little more than the building across the street.

"No, just make sure she doesn't leave. I'll be right out." Melissa hung up the phone, meeting Daniel's curious gaze with flashing blue eyes. "Come with me. I have to deal with something, and I think you may find it of interest."

Puzzled but intrigued, Daniel walked with Melissa outside to the fenced-in parking lot behind the redbrick loft building that housed the publishing company. There were about twenty cars in the small lot.

One of them was Rose Browning's Chevy Impala.

A uniformed security guard fell into step with them as they headed across the lot. "Is she dangerous?" he asked Melissa.

"I don't think so."

Daniel stared at Melissa's grim expression. "What the hell is going on?"

She didn't answer, striding forward as the driver-side door opened and Rose stepped from the car.

Rose's eyelids fluttered briefly as she looked at Melissa, almost like a flinch, Daniel noted with surprise.

"I told you to stay away from me," Melissa snapped.

Rose's chin came up. "Not in those exact words."

"Well, let me be clear. You need help. And, until you get it, I don't want you anywhere near me, my home or my business." Melissa folded her arms across her chest.

"I've already talked to the police about you. They know everything you told me. It'll take one call to get a restraining order."

Rose's lower lip trembled, but she didn't drop her gaze. "I just wanted to make sure you're okay."

"What's going on here?" Daniel asked.

Both women turned their gazes to him. Melissa's fiery, Rose's apprehensive.

Melissa was the first to answer. "There's something you don't know about Rose, Daniel." She looked at Rose. "Should you tell him or should I?"

Rose's gaze dropped, her hands trembling.

Melissa looked back at Daniel. "Yesterday, Rose informed me that I was going to die if I didn't get out of town."

Daniel frowned, not understanding. "What?"

"How'd you put it?" Melissa asked Rose. "Oh, yeah. She sees death."

Rose looked at him, her expression a mixture of anger and shame. But there was no sign of denial, no hint of refutation.

"You see death?" he repeated.

Her mouth tightened, her eyes locking with his. "Right now, Melissa's face is covered with a translucent image of itself. Sort of like a veil."

Daniel couldn't keep his gaze from shifting to Melissa's face. He saw nothing but her pretty, even features.

"You can't see it. Only I can."

"And that's all there is? The image of her face?" That made no sense, Daniel thought. None of this makes any sense.

Rose shook her head, her eyes welling with tears. "The death veil is covered with bloody slashes. Several crisscrossing gashes on her forehead and cheeks." Her voice weakened. "And her throat is slit."

Images flashed through Daniel's mind. Body after body, disfigured by a killer's escalating rage.

She was describing the marks of Orion.

Chapter Eight

Melissa held up her hand. "Enough. I want you off this property now or I'm calling the police."

Rose dragged her gaze from Daniel's narrowed eyes and looked at Melissa. "Okay. I'm going. But please, please be careful." She looked at Daniel again, trying to read his dark expression. He was skeptical, obviously. Thrown by the whole thing. But she'd seen something else in his eyes.

Recognition.

She had described the killer's handiwork perfectly, and he knew it.

"This is why I called you here, Daniel," Melissa said, her voice low with anger. "To warn you about Rose." She hooked her arm through Daniel's, turning to the nearby security guard. When she spoke, her voice was cold. "See that she leaves."

Daniel turned away, walking back to the building with Melissa. The security guard held his ground, his grim look making Rose's stomach hurt.

She returned to her Chevy and slid behind the steering wheel, gripping the wheel with shaking hands before fumbling her key into the ignition.

Okay, so coming here wasn't a good idea.

But she couldn't bear sitting at home, wondering if Melissa was even still alive. Though there'd been no report of a new murder on the news, she'd figured it was possible that the body just hadn't been found yet. She'd tried all the numbers she had for Melissa, without any response.

She'd panicked, pure and simple. Acted before she thought. And now she'd paid a high price for her impulsiveness.

Daniel knew.

It had been foolish to think she could keep secret something so elemental to who she was, not if she wanted to use the death veils to make a difference in the lives of people at risk. She knew she could make a difference, if only someone believed her. But nobody believed her. Especially not Daniel.

She was on her own.

DANIEL STARED at the narrow road illuminated by the Jeep's headlights, his mind still in the parking lot of Bannerman Publishing, reliving the scene between Rose and Melissa over and over again in hopes of making sense of what seemed nonsensical.

There was no chance Rose Browning was telling the truth. It was only a question of whether she was lying or crazy.

Daniel's dealings with her argued against the latter; she held a job, paid a mortgage and was able to communicate clearly and rationally, so insanity wasn't the answer.

But why would she have chosen such a crazy-sounding lie to explain her insider knowledge of Orion's modus operandi?

He shouldn't have gone back inside with Melissa after the parking lot scene. He should have followed Rose home immediately, caught her with her guard down and her emotions running high and gotten to the bottom of her deception. Instead, he'd given her several hours to calm down, to rethink her plan and come up with a different excuse.

Couldn't be helped now, he thought grimly, pulling the Jeep onto Twentieth Street. She'd still be caught off guard to find him at her door at eight-thirty on a Thursday night.

Five Points South teemed with people taking advantage of the mild October night. He passed the Southside Pub's neon-lit entrance, a reminder of his first encounter with Rose Browning. Wearing something sleek and red, her dark hair gathered in a neat coil at the base of her neck, she'd made an impact.

He stopped at the traffic light by the Storyteller fountain, his mind still replaying that first, brief meeting. No words exchanged, only a look that had set a fire in his belly, a need that lingered, unquenched, even now.

Whether she was a liar or not.

Lost in memory, he barely registered the small group of pedestrians crossing the street in front of him until a dark-haired beauty in a short black skirt and leather jacket dragged his attention back to the present. It took a second to realize she wasn't a figment of his imagination, conjured up by his preoccupation with Rose Browning and her secrets.

It was Rose herself, dressed for clubbing in a flippy little skirt that hit her midthigh, exposing long, toned legs made sexier by a pair of spike-heeled pumps. Tonight she wore her hair down in sleek, dark waves that framed her heart-shaped face. She walked apart from the rest of the smiling, laughing pedestrians, her expression tense and focused.

As she reached the sidewalk on the other side of the street, the light changed. Daniel flicked on his turn signal and made a right onto a side road, following her.

He drove slowly, staying just behind her as she strode toward a pair of bars near the end of the block. She entered the nearest one: Sizzle. The bar where Alice Donovan had spent her last night on earth.

Scanning the street for a parking place and finding none, Daniel settled on the side lot next to Hannity's, the Irish pub next door. He didn't enter Sizzle immediately; he had a feeling she'd be watching the door. Instead, he waited outside Hannity's, pretending to read the dinner menu posted on the window, until a crowd of six young men approached the entrance to the dance club. Daniel fell in behind them, using them as cover until he was safely through the front door.

He peeled off, disappearing into the dim belly of the club, well away from the dance floor or the long maple bar near the far wall. Settling at a table near one corner, he scanned the club until he spotted Rose standing near the bar. Her gaze moved around the room, restive and alert.

Who was she looking for? Orion?

Daniel's pulse quickened, anticipation battling dread in his gut. Did she know who Orion was? Was she here to meet him, to help him pick out his next prey? Was it possible?

He wished he could believe she was insane instead. Something loud and driving played over the club's speakers, an electronic mating call to the twentysome-things grinding and gyrating on the dance floor. He watched Rose, wondering if she'd venture from the bar and start mingling with the crowd.

Maybe she'd just come here to pick up a date, he told himself, trying to ignore the rush of acid in his gut. She was single, young and pretty. She wouldn't be the only woman in this place looking for a warm body to share a bed with tonight.

If she were any other woman and he were any other man, he might offer himself for the job.

A smiling redhead walked slowly past his table, blocking his view of Rose. He looked up to find the woman watching him, invitation in her blue eyes. He smiled politely but looked away, trying to reacquire his target.

She was no longer at the bar.

Standing, he tried to spot her among the writhing throng on the dance floor. But she wasn't there.

As a waitress moved his way, he headed for the front door and emerged into the cool night, the thud-ding beat of the music from the club echoing the pulse in his ears.

"Lose something?"

He turned to find Rose leaning against the club's weathered brick facade, her pale brown eyes glittering.

He didn't try to lie. "Yes. You."

Her lips curved. "Afraid I might accost some other poor woman and loose my insanity on her?"

"Never said you were insane."

"You didn't have to." Rose pushed away from the wall. "How did you know I'd be here?"

"I didn't. I was on my way to your house and spotted you crossing near the fountain."

"You were on your way to my house? Why?"

"Did you think I'd just leave things the way they were at Melissa's office?"

"Actually, yes." Rose started walking down the sidewalk, heading toward Twentieth Street.

Daniel caught her arm. "My car's parked in the lot next door. Let me drive you back to your car."

"Who says I'm going back to my car?"

He tightened his grip on her arm. "You, of all people, should know it's not safe for a woman to be walking around Five Points South by herself at night." Leaning closer, he lowered his voice. "Unless there's some reason you believe you have nothing to fear."

Her eyes darkened with dismay. "You think I know who the killer is? You think I'm working with him or something? My God, Daniel." Dismay shifted to revulsion. She pulled her arm from his grasp. "I'd rather you believe I was crazy." She headed toward the intersection with Twentieth Street.

Daniel caught up with her. "Those are the two options, aren't they? You're either crazy or a liar."

"Or I'm telling the truth."

"I gave up believing in magic in second grade."

"It's not magic." She wobbled as her heel hit a crack in the sidewalk.

He caught her arm, steadying her. A buzz of energy crackled through his fingertips and shimmied up his arm. "Then, what is it?"

She stopped in the middle of the sidewalk, gazing up at him with haunted eyes. "It's a curse."

He didn't know what to say in response. If she were telling the truth, if she could see the things she said she could, of course she'd feel that way. He understood the feeling; he'd often wondered what kind of darkness in his soul allowed him to visualize the workings of a sick, depraved mind, to predict and anticipate the most evil of acts.

She started to pull her arm away again, but he held on. "I assume you're not here to pick up a date for the night," he murmured. "So why the club hopping?"

She looked down. "I was looking for Melissa."

He tipped her chin up, forcing her to meet his gaze. "She told you to stay away from her. I don't think she was kidding. She could get a restraining order if you push this."

Her chin jutted forward, sliding deeper into his palm. "Bars are public places."

"Why did you think she'd be here?"

"She'd told me she and Mark were going to celebrate their third anniversary of dating by going out tonight, and I remembered that she'd said they'd met at Sizzle. I just hoped—"

"You'd find them here?"

Rose nodded.

He dropped his hand away from her face before he heeded his body's clamoring to pull her into his arms. "And then what?"

She didn't answer right away, piquing his curiosity. But standing in the middle of the sidewalk as they were, they were beginning to attract attention, so he pressed his hand to the small of her back and nudged her toward the parking lot where he'd left his Jeep. "Let me drive you home, Rose, and we can talk about this some more."

"I'm not stalking her," Rose said, even as she let him move her toward the parking lot.

"Then, what would you call it?"

She paused at the parking-lot entrance. "Let's say—just for kicks—I see what I say I do. And that the death veils mean what I think they do. That would mean Melissa's life is in danger, and she's on the killer's target list, right?"

He nudged her toward the Jeep.

"Then, Orion could be out here, right now, where she is. Looking for her just like I am. And if I find her, I might be able to spot him."

"And do what?"

"Call the police."

He nodded. "And tell them what? That you've seen death veils on Melissa Bannerman and because some poor guy just happened to be watching her inappropriately, golly gee, he just has to be the killer?"

Her mouth tightened. "Those weren't the words I'd planned to use, no."

"It'll sound the same to any cop on the street, Rose."

"Fine. You don't approve of what I'm doing." She stopped at the rear of his Jeep. "I didn't ask you to chaperone me."

"And that was your first mistake. Since we're still pretending you really do see death veils, what makes you think the killer won't come after you?"

"I looked in the rearview mirror before I got out of the car," she answered, her gaze steady.

The certainty in her voice unnerved him. Maybe he'd ruled out insanity too quickly.

She looked away. "I know this makes you uncomfortable—"

"I've interviewed men who've disemboweled their victims," he said more harshly than he'd intended, making her flinch. "I can handle hearing about your visions."

"I'm just saying, I'm not the one in danger."

"Maybe not from Orion," he conceded. "But there are other predators walking these streets."

Her expression shifted, as if that thought hadn't occurred to her. But she squared her shoulders. "I stay in crowded places. I buy nonalcoholic drinks and never let them out of my sight. And I know better than to trust a stranger."

"What if Orion's not a stranger? Could be anyone. Hell, I could be Orion for all you know."

She angled a look at him. "And you want me to get into your car in a dark parking lot?"

Touché.

She held his gaze a moment, her expression serious. Then her lips curved slightly. "I don't think you're him."

"You're lucky I was the one who spotted you."

"Because this is where Orion chooses his victims?"

"Or stalks them." He opened the passenger door for her. "Several of his past victims were last seen at bars. He sees places like this as his hunting ground. He spots his prey, stalks her and catches her when she's tipsy or tired, and somehow he convinces her to let her guard down with him."

"How?" Sounding curious, Rose slid into the Jeep's passenger seat and buckled herself in.

"If I knew that, I'd be a lot closer to finding him," Daniel answered, sliding behind the wheel. As he reached for his seat belt, his cell phone vibrated against his hip.

He pulled the phone from his pocket and read the display panel. The number was local but unfamiliar. He shut the phone off, letting the call go to his message box.

"Need to get that?" she asked.

He shook his head. "I'll check the voice mail later." He backed the Jeep out of the parking lot.

She directed him across Twentieth Street to a shadowy side street. Her Impala was one of a half-dozen cars parked there, taking advantage of free weekend parking. He squelched a shudder at the thought of her walking down that darkened street for a couple of blocks before she got anywhere near bright lights and the safety of a crowd.

He let her out next to her car, catching her wrist as she reached for her seat-belt buckle. "Don't ever park on a street like this at night, even if you're not alone. It's asking for trouble."

Her sober gaze met his. "Okay."

He let go of her wrist and watched until she was safely locked inside her car. Backing up, he gave her room to pull out of the parking place.

He stayed close, following her back to her house on Mountain Avenue. When she pulled into the alley and parked in a gravel drive behind her house, he pulled in behind her. Even if it was playing with fire, he wasn't going to let her go into that empty house alone.

She waited for him at the top of the wooden steps leading down the sloping yard to her back door. "You sure you aren't a frustrated bodyguard at heart?"

He laid his hand on her back. "Want me to leave?"

She shook her head. "But I promise I'll look into getting an alarm system put in first thing tomorrow so you don't have to worry so much about me."

He doubted even an alarm system would make him stop worrying about her. Whatever had put her front and center in the Orion murder case, she wouldn't be safe until he was caught or moved on to the next town. "I'll take a look around to make sure everything's okay."

She nodded her approval but didn't make a move to follow him. Squelching a pang of disappointment, he checked all the rooms and returned downstairs. He found Rose still in the kitchen, standing near the back door. She reached for the door handle. "Thanks for checking things out."

He frowned. "You're kicking me out?"

She gave him a look of surprise. "You thought we were making a date of this?"

Ouch. "Actually, I thought it might be a good idea if I stayed tonight."

Her eyebrow darted higher.

"On the sofa," he added. "Frustrated bodyguard, remember?"

A nervous chuckle escaped her throat. "I don't think it's necessary."

"Humor me."

Her half smile faded to a frown. "I'm more worried about Melissa than me."

"She's with her fiancé, isn't she?"

Her frown only deepened, piquing his curiosity.

"There something about her fiancé I should know?"

She cleared her expression. "They've had…issues." Her mouth tightened, making it clear she would say no more. But he could make an educated guess. Nothing like an impending wedding to make a groom-to-be start panicking about the whole "until death do us part" thing.

As he well knew.

She nodded toward the kitchen table. "Want something to drink? I don't have anything alcoholic around here—"

"Whatever you have is fine." He sat at the table and reached into his pocket for his cell phone to see if his mystery caller had left a message.

"Daniel? It's Melissa Bannerman." Her recorded voice sounded raspy. He heard a sniffling sound as she took a breath. "I know we're mostly strangers, but I need a ride home."

He sat forward, instantly alert.

"I'm in Trussville," she continued, referring to a suburb east of Birmingham. Though teary-sounding, Melissa's voice oozed disgust. "Mark and I had a fight. I should've known something was up when he wanted to come out here. Maybe the bastard thought his little tramp of a girlfriend wouldn't be able to track him down if he changed his patterns. Idiot!"

Her fiancé was two-timing her and Melissa had found out about it, Daniel interpreted.

"I wasn't going to get in the car with him after that," she added. "And I really don't feel up to hearing any of my friends or family say 'I told you so' tonight, you know? Call me back? I really need a ride home." The message ended with a click.

Daniel pushed the return call button on his phone. Melissa answered on the first ring. "Hello?"

"It's Daniel. You okay?"

Rose turned at the sound of his voice, her eyebrows cocked. He gave her an apologetic look.

She sniffled. "No. I just left the restaurant and started walking, I was so angry. I know that was stupid."

"Where are you now?" Daniel looked up as Rose brought the two glasses of juice to the table. She met his gaze, her expression curious.

"On Highway 11 somewhere," Melissa answered his question, sniffling. "I'm past where all the stores and houses are. It's really dark here."

What the hell was she thinking? "You need to head back toward the restaurant. I don't care if the jerk is there, you need to be around people—"

There was a clicking sound in his ear, and he heard Melissa utter a soft curse. "Battery—" She managed to get the word out before the connection broke.

"Melissa?" Apprehension slithered through his belly.

"What's going on?" Rose's voice was low and tight.

"Melissa and her fiancé had an argument, and she walked out of the restaurant where they were eating." He disconnected and punched in her number again, waiting for a ring. Her voice mail message came up immediately.

"Walked out? By herself?" Rose looked horrified. "What was she thinking?"

"I don't think she was thinking at all," Daniel admitted. "Where is she?"

"Highway 11 west of Trussville."

Rose's eyes widened even more. "Go get her. Now."

"You're coming with me," he decided, already moving toward the back door.

"She won't be happy to see me," Rose warned, but she sounded relieved that he was including her in the trip.

"She'll deal," Daniel told her as she locked up.

His mind racing, he calculated the distance and time. Five minutes to the Red Mountain Expressway, ten to I-59 north. From there, it was a twenty-minute drive to the Trussville exit. Just thirty minutes. All Melissa had to do was get somewhere safe and stay there for thirty minutes, and he'd be there to take her safely home. Fortunately, Trussville was miles away from Southside, where Orion seemed to do all of his hunting. Melissa should be safe from him.

But Orion wasn't the only bad guy around.

WHY MELISSA HADN'T CALLED a cab the minute she stormed out of the restaurant, he didn't know. Instead, she'd begun walking back toward Birmingham, her strides angry and determined. It was the wrong direction to have chosen, heading away from lights and people down a road that wasn't all that well traveled thanks to the interstate that ran parallel through the growing suburb.

It suited his purposes.

He followed, passing her and parking a mile down the highway in an area where streetlights were widely spaced and the traffic was light. He knew she'd keep walking away from the restaurant, away from the humiliating scene that had shattered her idyllic little fantasy of happily-ever-after.

Fifteen minutes later, he spotted her coming toward him, her gait wobbly in those spiky high heels she loved so much. She was punching buttons on her cell phone, her body language communicating despair rather than the anger that had propelled her from the restaurant earlier. He gripped the wheel, waiting. He couldn't make his move while she was on the phone.

There. She thrust her phone into the little bag hanging from her shoulder on a thin strap and turned around, heading back up the highway toward Trussville.

A quick scan of the highway reassuring him that there weren't any cars to witness his next move, he pulled onto the highway behind her. She turned toward him as he came level with her, her eyes squinting against the glare of his headlights. She took a step back on the shoulder, nearly falling as the heel of her shoe sank into the sandy soil.

He lowered the passenger-side window and turned on the dome light so she could see his face. Her wary expression shifted to recognition.

Exactly as planned.

Chapter Nine

"Yes, that sounds like her." The restaurant manager's voice was tight with disapproval. "We don't normally have those sorts of scenes in a place like this."

Rose looked up at Daniel's tense expression, her stomach aching with fear. They'd been up and down the highway for the past half hour with no sign of Melissa. They'd gone from restaurant to restaurant until they'd found Chez Sofie and someone who remembered Melissa being there that evening.

"She didn't come back here?" Daniel asked.

"No. Her…companions left soon after she did, and I haven't seen either of them since." He looked pleased by that fact, as if his restaurant had been spared further ignominy.

Daniel sighed. "You remember anyone else leaving the restaurant soon after Ms. Bannerman left?"

"Only the gentleman and the other lady." The manager turned away from them dismissively, pasting a smile on his face as he greeted a couple coming through the front doors. "Welcome to Chez Sofie. Do you have a reservation?"

Daniel touched Rose's back, nodding toward the exit. They emerged into the cool night air, Rose's heart hammering hard against her breast.

"Maybe Mark found her and talked her into letting him drive her home." Daniel opened the Jeep door for her.

"Why didn't she call you back on his phone, then? To let you know you didn't have to come?" She slid into the seat, searching his face for a hint of hope.

Though he tried to keep his expression neutral, she didn't miss the grim set of his mouth. "Don't know," he admitted.

She buckled her seat belt and laid her head back against the headrest. "I don't have Mark's cell-phone number on my cell phone, but I think I have it in my address book back at home." She bit her lip. "Why didn't I think to bring it with me?"

"Because you had no idea you'd need to call him," Daniel said sensibly, strapping in and starting the Jeep. "Can we go back down Highway 11?" she asked as he started toward the interstate. "Just in case?"

"Sure," he agreed. But he didn't sound hopeful.

They reached Roebuck without spotting Melissa anywhere along the highway. Daniel slanted a look at Rose. "Odds really are that she met up with Mark and he took her home."

"You don't believe that."

"It's the most likely answer," he insisted.

She turned to look at him. His profile was outlined by the indigo glow of the dashboard lights, his jaw squared and tight. "But you don't really believe it," she repeated softly.

He glanced at her again, not answering.

"It's a gut feeling," she added. "Nothing scientific or logical. Just a little voice inside your head telling you that the most likely answer isn't the right one. Right?"

His jaw muscle bunched.

"He has her." Rose voiced her deepest fear, certain it was true. "There's nothing we can do to stop him from killing her."

"Until we have more information to go on, let's not think the worst. Okay?"

She settled against the seat, her heart a painful knot in her chest. Intellectually, she knew he was right. Until they talked to Mark, they couldn't be sure of anything. But in her gut, she knew. The man Daniel called Orion had Melissa, and he wasn't going to drop her off safely at home tonight.

The only questions were, where would he leave her body and when would it be found?

DANIEL LISTENED to the muted chatter on the police radio sitting on Rose's side table, trying not to think the worst. He hadn't been able to reach Melissa on her cell phone or at home, and Mark Phagan wasn't answering either of the numbers Rose had in her address book. Calling the police so early was pointless, especially since Melissa had ample reason to be lying low after whatever had happened between her and Mark at the restaurant.

Rose had settled into a restless doze around 2:00 a.m., curled into a half-fetal position on her sofa. She looked young and vulnerable, her face soft with sleep. He felt the urge to scoop her up in his arms, carry her up the stairs to her bedroom and settle her under the colorful quilt.

And it was a toss-up whether he'd tuck her in or join her under the covers.

He was crazy to be thinking of her this way. He still didn't have a clue how she knew so much about Orion and his murders. Getting any more involved with her before he'd settled that question was criminally stupid.

But she couldn't have feigned the fear he'd seen in her eyes when she realized Melissa was really missing. She hadn't faked the troubled dreams that had chased her for the last two hours, making her toss and turn on the sofa, low sounds of distress trapped in her throat.

He slouched in the chair, allowing himself to memorize the curve of her jaw, the soft bow of her lips, the brush of her long, dark lashes against her cheeks. The makeup she'd worn to go clubbing was mostly gone, save for the smudge of mascara darkening the skin beneath her eyes. And, yet, in that perfect moment in time, he knew he'd never seen anything more beautiful in his life.

But perfect moments always came to an end, and his ended at 4:21 a.m., when the call came over the police scanner. Ten fifty-four—possible dead body. He pulled a notebook from his breast pocket and jotted down the address, waiting with growing apprehension for more information to come over the scanner.

Ten minutes later, the call came, confirming the dead body and calling for the coroner.

Daniel looked across the living room at Rose's sleeping form, his heart sinking. The last thing he wanted to do was to wake her when all he knew was that some poor soul had died that night. But he couldn't bring himself to sneak out and leave her here to wonder what had happened.

He woke her with a gentle shake. Her eyes fluttered open and settled on him, her gaze warm and liquid. For a moment, he almost let himself forget the murders, the call on the scanner, everything but the raw need he saw simmering in the depths of her mossy-brown eyes. But she looked away, breaking the connection. Her gaze flew to the scanner on the side table. "Has something happened?"

He told her about the police call, trying to hide his own growing uneasiness as he told her that it could be a death completely unconnected to Melissa or Orion himself. "I thought I'd head to the scene and see what I could find out."

"I'm coming with you." She untangled her legs from the knit throw and sat up.

"Rose, you shouldn't go. I don't know what I'll find—"

"I can't stay here and worry. I'll stay in the car while you check on it, but please don't make me stay here."

Knowing futility when he saw it, he nodded. "But you stay in the car."

"Thank you." Relief and dread mingled in her voice. "I'll go change clothes."

She returned a few minutes later, her hair in a pony-tail and her face scrubbed clean. She'd changed out of her club clothes into a moss-green sweater and a pair of faded jeans. "Ready?" she asked.

Not really, he thought. But he gave a nod and fol-lowed her outside, where the early morning quiet was broken by the faint hum of traffic on the expressway a few blocks away.

For most of the city, life went on, oblivious to the fact that a woman lay dead only a few blocks away.

WAITING IN THE CAR was only marginally better than waiting at home, Rose decided as the hand on her wristwatch clicked past 5:00 a.m. Daniel had left the Jeep about fifteen minutes ago, disappearing into the small clump of bystanders gathered outside the yellow crime-scene tape cordoning off an overgrown, empty lot that had once been a school playground. The abandoned school loomed in the background, shuttered and silent, its dark facade painted blue and crimson by the flashing dome lights of the police cruisers parked at haphazard angles along the curb.

Rose reached into her purse for her cell phone, hitting the speed dial for Melissa's home phone. After six rings, the answering machine picked up. Rose hung up before the beep; Daniel had already left a message on her machine last night.

She tried Mark Phagan's home number with the same result. Grimacing with frustration, she put her phone on the seat beside her, peering through the Jeep's windshield to see if she could catch a glimpse of Daniel in the crowd. Time slowed to a mind-numbing crawl, each minute interminable.

On impulse, she picked up her phone and tried Melissa's cell-phone number one more time. It rang three times, then there was a click. But no one spoke.

"Melissa? It's me—please don't hang up—"

More silence.

Rose's heart began pounding. "Melissa?"

"Who is this?" a man's voice asked.

Rose's heart skipped a beat. A cold chill washed over her, making her light-headed and shaky. Her vision narrowed to a pinpoint.

It must be him. He'd killed Melissa and taken her cell phone—

"Hello?" the voice repeated. "I asked, who is this?"

"Who is this?" she countered, forcing the words from her constricted throat.

There was a brief pause, then the man answered, "This is Detective Frank Carter with the Birmingham Police Department."

Relief shuddered through her, quickly swallowed by despair. If Detective Carter had Melissa's phone—

"I told you who I am. It's your turn."

She licked her lips. "It's Rose Browning. Melissa's friend."

Detective Carter released a slow, deep breath. "Oh. I'm sorry to tell you this, Ms. Browning, but your friend is dead."

Rose closed her eyes, pain closing around her throat. Even though she'd spent the last hours preparing for this moment, it hit her like a truck. She tried to say something but only a strangled bleat escaped her mouth.

"I'm very sorry for your loss," Detective Carter said, his voice gentle. "I'll want to speak to you later, so don't leave town in the next few days, okay?"

"Okay." She managed to get the word out.

"I'll talk to you soon." He hung up.

Rose dropped her phone to her lap, sinking back against the seat. A shiver shook her, scattering chill bumps across her arms and chest. She wrapped her arms over her chest, trying to control the tremors.

The trill of her cell phone split the silence of the Jeep's cab. She jumped, the phone tumbling to the floorboard. She groped for it in the darkness. "Hello?"

"It's me." Daniel's voice rumbled through her, warm and solid, easing her shivers. "How're you holding up?"

She could tell by his careful tone that he already knew about Melissa. "I know it's her," she said. "I tried Melissa's cell phone and Detective Carter answered."

Daniel sighed. "That was a terrible way to hear it."

"There's no good way to hear it." She closed her eyes, her head beginning to ache. "Have you learned anything else?"

"Not yet. I'm hoping to get Frank off by himself to see what I can learn without the feds catching wind of my interest."

Rose caught sight of Daniel through the windshield. He stood near the edge of the crowd gathered behind the police cars, his cell phone to his ear. Just seeing him, knowing he was close, eased some of her tension. "I see you," she murmured, her voice tinged with unexpected tenderness.

He turned and looked toward her. "I see you, too." The low, intimate tone of his voice set a fire in her belly, radiating warmth through her chilled limbs. "You have the doors locked, don't you?"

She eyed the door locks. "Yes."

"Keep your eyes open, okay? If you see anyone heading your direction, call me immediately. You have my number?"

"Yes," she assured him.

He didn't say anything for a moment, just stared down the street at her. When he spoke, his voice softened. "We have a lot to talk about when we're through here."

"I know."

"I've got to go see if I can get Frank to tell me anything. Don't forget—call me if anyone starts to approach you."

"I won't forget."

"I'm sorry about Melissa," he said. "I'll be there as soon as I can." He rang off, weaving through the crowd again.

Rose clutched the phone to her chest, his warm voice lingering in her ears.

DANIEL EDGED HIS WAY to the police-tape cordon, trying to catch Frank Carter's eye. When Frank glanced his way, Daniel gestured at him. Carter's expression darkened, his mouth tightening with annoyance, but he said something to the detective standing next to him and headed toward the street.

Frank didn't make eye contact with Daniel as he lifted the crime scene tape and ducked under it, but he gave a slight nod that Daniel took as an invitation to talk.

As Frank opened the trunk of an unmarked Oldsmobile Cutlass, Daniel joined him. "Number four?"

Frank didn't answer. Daniel didn't need him to. What he'd seen of Melissa's body confirmed it for him.

"I'd like to come in on the case officially," Daniel continued.

Frank slanted a dark look at him. "As what? A roving university professor?"

Daniel let the barb slide. "The last time we talked, you offered to speak to your boss about bringing me into the case."

"Last time, you said no."

"You think I'm going to horn in on your publicity when you catch this guy? I'm not. I don't want publicity. I just want this bastard to go down."

Frank stopped pretending to look for something in the car trunk and turned to face Daniel. "I've been doing a little investigating of my own, Danny. Tell me— what made you leave the FBI six years ago? Just felt the need to slow down, stop and smell the roses?"

Daniel could tell Frank knew the answer. "You know why."

Frank's voice darkened. "It's all about Tina, isn't it?"

Not all of it. But enough. "The FBI wanted me to move onto other cases six years ago, so I quit and took the university job. Might as well put the Ph.D. to work."

"You think this is the same guy?" Frank looked troubled.

"The M.O. is the same. The victims are similar— young, pretty women."

"What if you're just seeing what you want to see?"

Daniel didn't reply, no longer certain he knew the answer. If Frank, of all people, didn't see it—

Frank closed the trunk. Without turning around, he asked, "How did you know to be here this morning?"

"Police scanner."

"You were up at four in the morning listening to the police scanner?"

Daniel saw no reason not to tell Frank about Melissa's

call. He'd learn the truth once he checked the numbers on Melissa's cell phone, anyway. "Melissa had a fight with her boyfriend, and she left a message on my cell phone to see if I could come pick her up and take her home. But when I went looking for her, I couldn't find her."

Frank half turned, cutting his eyes at Daniel. "Why you? Is there something I need to know about you and Melissa Bannerman?"

"I told you before, she and I have been discussing a book."

Frank shook his head. "But why call you and not a friend? Or family?"

"She said she didn't want to get into it with people she knew. I get the feeling it's not the first trouble she's had with the fiancé."

"We'll be checking him out," Frank assured him. "Where was she when she called?"

Daniel told Frank everything he knew, leaving out only Rose's involvement. He was reluctant to put her on Frank's "persons of interest" list, at least until he'd settled for himself exactly what her connection to the case really was.

"I'll put out feelers with my captain about getting you involved," Frank said grudgingly. "But it won't be a paid position, and you can't be going off on a wild hare and screwing up our case. Understand?"

"Of course," Daniel said, not meaning it. He didn't need the locals to tell him how to investigate a case.

"Get lost, will you?" Frank muttered as he headed back under the crime-scene tape.

Daniel took his advice, drifting back through the

crowd and emerging on the other side. He walked slowly back down the street to his Jeep, squinting against the glare of the morning sun reflected in his front windshield.

He reached the driver's side door and looked inside. Rose's dark gaze met his through the glass, her expression a heady blend of relief and something that sent his pulse racing. She reached across and unlocked his door. "Any more news?"

Sliding behind the steering wheel, he told her about his conversation with Frank, leaving out the part about Tina. He never talked about Tina, hadn't in ten years. No point in starting now; it would just further muddle the already complicated relationship between him and Rose.

"I think he'll be able to get me officially in on the investigation," he added, buckling his seat belt.

"Is that good?" she asked as he started the engine.

"I'll have better access to the files on the past four victims." Not that he expected to see anything in those files he hadn't seen dozens of times before, but it was possible Orion had changed his tactics in a way that might reveal more about him than Daniel already knew.

At this point, he'd take any new information he could get.

"I should have warned her," Rose murmured.

"I thought you did."

"Not about the death veils. About Mark."

He sat forward. "What about Mark?"

"I knew there was a good chance he was cheating on her again, but I never told her. Maybe if I had—"

"Why didn't you?"

"Because I didn't have any proof. All I had was a snippet of conversation I'd overheard." She told him about hearing Mark Phagan set up an alibi with his friends at Alice's funeral. "I told myself he might have been planning a surprise for her or something, that it wasn't proof he was cheating. But I knew better." Misery tinged her voice.

Ignoring all the warning bells in his head, he took her hand in his. "Don't blame yourself about that. Might not have changed anything. Melissa said on the phone that she wouldn't listen to her friends when they tried to warn her about Mark."

"I know you think I'm crazy." Her voice was soft and sleepy. "Sometimes I think I am, too."

Which meant she wasn't, he thought. The really crazy ones never realized it. So she wasn't crazy. And she wasn't a liar. Which left one unthinkable explanation.

She really did see death veils.

His head ached. He'd been awake for twenty-four hours, much of that time spent wound like a spring. The last thing he needed to do right now was to try to make sense of the senseless.

He parked behind Rose's house. When they reached the house, he took the keys from her trembling hands and unlocked the door. "Get some sleep. It's going to be a long day."

She lifted shadowed eyes to his. "For you, too."

"I have a few calls I need to make, but I'll catch a quick nap on your sofa when I'm through, if that's okay."

As Rose headed upstairs, Daniel called his research

assistant, Steve, whose groggy voice reminded Daniel that it was only 7:00 a.m. on a Sunday morning. "Sorry to wake you, Steve, but I have a new murder to add to the running tally."

That woke Steve up a bit. "Number four?"

Daniel outlined the facts in the Melissa Bannerman murder. "I've never been this close."

"You've never made it to a place while Orion's still active there," Steve pointed out.

"He got sloppy this time, killing them all in one area."

"Except the last one."

There was that, Daniel had to admit. While the killer had dumped Melissa in the same general area as the others, he'd picked her up well across town. "We've figured all along that these weren't murders of opportunity."

"He stalks them," Steve agreed.

Still, he had gone outside his comfort zone last night when he'd targeted Melissa. Maybe he'd made a mistake. All the more reason to join the investigation in an official capacity.

He rang off with Steve and dialed the number for the Birmingham Police Department Homicide Bureau. The captain was out of her office, no doubt still front and center at the crime scene, but he left her a voice mail to get the ball rolling.

Finished with his calls, Daniel headed upstairs to check on Rose. The next few days were going to be hell for her, dealing with the aftermath of Melissa's murder, and he didn't know how much time he could spend with her if he managed to convince the police to bring him into the investigation on a more official basis. He'd probably be putting in long hours studying the case files and catching himself up on all the details.

Rose's bedroom door was open just enough for him to see her slim figure stretched out atop the covers of her bed. Through the window beyond, dawn painted the Birmingham skyline in shades of saffron and coral.

He'd kissed Rose in front of that window, he thought, the memory vivid enough to send his heart racing. He felt the pull of her, even now, a tidal pulse of need.

He crossed quietly to her bedside. She'd taken a shower and changed into a long-sleeved T-shirt and a pair of flannel pajama bottoms. Her hair was damp, and the air around her smelled like a fresh sea breeze, tangy-sweet. He breathed deeply, memorizing the scent.

He eased a nearby armchair next to the bed and sat, studying her sleep-softened features. The morning light bathed her face with warmth, burnishing the smooth apples of her cheeks. His fingers ached to touch her, but he resisted, reminding himself that she was still a puzzle that needed solving, a key piece of the mystery he'd spent the last years of his life trying to unravel.

Letting her mean anything more to him than that was a mistake he couldn't afford to make.

HE FOLDED THE NOTE carefully, the latex gloves a minor nuisance. Part of him longed to touch the paper, to know his flesh had touched something Rose would touch, but he wasn't insane. She'd take the note to the police for testing. So he took care; used bottled water to seal the envelope. He ran a hand vac over both note and envelope before sealing the first inside the second. The envelope immediately went into a resealable plastic bag for the trip.

He felt flush, still sated by what he had done. He wasn't delusional like some who did what he did; he didn't imagine himself ridding the earth of harlots or releasing tortured souls from hell on earth into eternal paradise. He killed because he liked to watch the aftermath. Like a stone hitting the surface of a placid lake, what he did sent out circles of reaction, and he liked to see just how far those circles could travel. It started small—the victim, her loved ones, her friends. With a single act, he'd changed the course of their lives forever.

But the effects of his handiwork didn't stop with those closest to her. They spread across the full spectrum of his victim's life, touching acquaintances, her neighborhood, even her city. Killing wasn't a solitary crime with a single victim. When he killed, his actions affected thousands of people in ways big and small.

It wasn't about sex. It wasn't about hate.

It was about power.

He had always been an arbitrary, greedy god over his chosen domain, striking when and where he pleased for reasons that made sense to no one but him.

But now he had Rose.

She would tell him who came next.

Chapter Ten

Unrelenting darkness swallowed Rose, as cold as death. Goose bumps scattered along her arms and legs, the skin at the back of her neck prickling with unease.

She wasn't alone in the darkness. She could hear him breathing, a slow, soft whisper of sound close by.

She turned in a slow circle, her eyes darting back and forth but finding nothing but blackness. But she still heard him breathing, so close that she imagined she could feel the warmth of his breath on her skin.

Terror trapped her own breath deep in her burning chest. Her head began to swim, specks of color sparkling in the blackness. She forced herself to breathe, trembling as sweet air rushed into her lungs.

A chuffing sound filled her ears. He was laughing at her.

"Who are you?" she rasped.

He didn't answer, but she felt his breath hot on her neck.

She whirled, flailing out and hitting only air. Her arm swung around and hit her side with a thud, making her gasp.

Twin circles of blinding light pierced the darkness. Rose squinted, her pupils contracting as the lights grew. A rumbling sound filled her ears, growing louder as the featureless darkness faded into recognizable shapes. She stood on the side of a dark highway, surrounded by trees and brush. The lights were car headlights moving toward her on the deserted road.

A narrow strip of grassy shoulder separated the highway from twin stands of young pines rising on either side of the road. Down the highway about a mile, the trees thinned out to make room for houses set well back from the road. Light from inside the homes dotted the darkness with specks of warm gold.

But they were too far away to hear her if she screamed.

The headlights filled her vision, driving out the darkness. She squinted, her eyes aching.

Suddenly the lights flickered out. The car came to a stop beside her, the engine noise idling down to a low growl.

She wanted to run, but her legs wouldn't move.

The driver's door opened. A dome light blinked on, backlighting the figure emerging from the car. She peered at him, trying to make out features, but he was only a silhouette.

"Who are you?" she asked again.

He didn't answer, moving with deliberate strides. One hand lifted, gripped around the shaft of a large hunting knife, its shiny steel blade reflecting the dome light's pale white glow.

Rose screamed.

The darkness exploded with light. Rose's legs came

to life, thrashing to free themselves of the strange paralysis that had gripped her in the darkness.

It took a moment to realize she was in her own bed, her legs tangled in a chenille throw. She fell back against her pillows, her pulse hammering in her throat. The events of the night before flooded her mind in a sickening rush.

Melissa was dead, she remembered, her heart leaden.

The bed shifted. Her eyes flew open to find Daniel beside her, his gray eyes warm with concern. "You screamed."

She covered her face, embarrassment warming her cheeks. "I had a nightmare."

He stroked her arm. "Obviously."

"I think I was imagining what Melissa must have seen." The glitter of the knife blade was clear in her mind. She met Daniel's gaze. "But I don't think I got it right."

He didn't speak, giving her an opening to continue.

"I was alone on a highway. It was pitch-black and deserted. I remember thinking nobody was close enough to hear me scream."

He brushed a strand of hair out of her face, his fingers sliding along the curve of her cheek. "Must've been scary."

"There was a car. It stopped beside me, and a man got out. I couldn't see his face, only the blade of his knife."

Daniel pulled her to him, sliding his hand up and down her back in a gentle, soothing motion. "I'm sorry."

"I don't think that's how it was for Melissa," she murmured against his neck. "I think she saw him and was relieved."

Daniel pulled back. "You think she knew him?"

"Do you think Melissa would go willingly with a stranger?"

"No," he conceded.

"I don't think Alice would have, either."

"So you think it was someone they both knew."

"Maybe it was Mark Phagan."

Daniel threaded his fingers through hers. "Because she found out he was cheating? Wouldn't his murder be the more likely outcome?"

"What if he's Orion?"

Daniel's eyebrows lifted. "Why would you think that?"

"We couldn't get him on his cell phone most of last night."

"He had a fiancée and a girlfriend both ready to kill him. He had a full plate."

"He lied to Melissa about where he was the night Alice Donovan died. He told Melissa he was going to Tuscaloosa, but I overheard him setting up an alibi with his friends."

Daniel glanced her way again. "Well, he was cheating on her. Maybe he lied to cover a tryst."

"What if he'd lied about something else?"

Daniel frowned. "Could explain Alice and Melissa, but what about the other two?"

"I don't know," she admitted. "Maybe Alice and Melissa were copycat killings."

"Melissa, maybe. But why Alice?"

She sighed, frustrated that she couldn't make her theory fit. "You're right. It doesn't make sense."

"Not if it's a copycat." He ran his thumb over the soft

skin of her wrist. "But maybe he knew the other victims, too."

"So he could be behind all four murders?"

"He'll be investigated. Significant others always are," Daniel assured her.

"What will that do to your theory about Orion?" Rose asked. "I can tell you right now, Mark has lived in Birmingham for the past six years, and he lived in Tuscaloosa before that. He wasn't traveling from state to state killing women."

Daniel frowned again. "So maybe I'm wrong about these killings. Maybe they're not the work of Orion."

"What happens if it's not? Do you move on?" Rose tried not to sound anxious, but the thought of him walking out of her life now hurt more than she'd expected.

He tangled his fingers in her damp hair, pulling her closer. He pressed his lips to her forehead. "We're a long way from this case being over. I'm not going anywhere."

He didn't add "for now," but the unspoken words rang in her head. She pulled him closer, tabling her doubts. He was with her now. That would have to be enough.

Daniel's fingers threaded through her hair, tugging her head up. He gazed into her eyes, as if searching for something just beyond his reach. "I'm sorry we didn't reach her in time."

The guilt in his voice pricked her eyes, eliciting tears. She blinked them back, afraid to give in to the grief hovering just beneath the surface of her emotions. No matter how her relationship with Melissa had ended, Rose had considered her a friend. Losing her, especially in such a violent way, was a wounding blow. But if she let herself cry, she wasn't sure she'd be able to stop.

Daniel brushed his mouth against hers, the touch soft and undemanding. A hot ache settled in the middle of her chest.

She wrapped her hand around the back of his neck and held him there, his lips still on hers. He tasted of mint toothpaste and smoky passion, sparking a hunger she'd never known before. She pulled back, gazing at his face as if she could will the true-love veil to appear. But she saw only his strong, masculine features, dark with a hint of curiosity.

"What's wrong?" he asked.

She shook her head wordlessly. He hesitated briefly, then tangled his fingers in her hair and tugged her toward him. He kissed her again, his hands sliding down her back to settle against her hips. He lifted her onto his lap, his hardness pressing against her softness.

She didn't care about the true-love veil, she realized. She just needed to forget. Forget death, fear or anything but the feel of heated flesh and whispered sighs.

Daniel groaned deep in his chest and laid her back against the pillows, his hips settling between her thighs. He kissed her throat, nipping the sensitive flesh. "Rose," he murmured.

She arched her back, liquid heat pooling low in her belly. She tugged the tails of his shirt from his waistband. His belt buckle dug into the flesh of her belly, a reminder that he was still wearing entirely too many clothes.

A ringing sound buzzed on the edge of her receding

consciousness, pesky as a fly. She tried to ignore it, reaching for Daniel's belt, but he stilled her hands.

"Someone's at the door." He rolled away from her.

She tugged at his arm, trying to pull him back to her. "They'll go away."

"Not if it's the police." Daniel sat up, combing his fingers through his tousled hair. He stood and tucked his shirttail into his trousers again. "We'd better check."

Rose released a frustrated growl and rolled off the bed. She grabbed the cotton bathrobe hanging on the back of her door.

She padded downstairs ahead of Daniel and peeked through the fish-eye lens in the front door. A distorted image of Detective Frank Carter looked back at her.

She patted her hair smooth and opened the door.

Frank stood in the doorway, a frown on his face. In his rubber-glove-encased right hand he held a small white envelope.

Rose's heart skipped a beat.

"This was propped against the door when I arrived." Frank looked past Rose at Daniel, one eyebrow inching upward. "I need a plastic bag."

As Daniel disappeared into the house, Rose scanned the quiet neighborhood, the hair on her arms prickling. Traffic was light this early, a car or two passing while she watched. Three houses down, a neighbor dressed in a sweatsuit walked her poodle around her small front yard.

So ordinary, untouched by the violence that lurked nearby.

She could feel him nearby. He wanted to see her

open the envelope, to see her expression when she read the message inside.

Daniel returned with a plastic sandwich bag. He held it open so Frank could drop the envelope into the bag.

Rose peered at the envelope. There was nothing on the envelope, not even her name.

"Same as last time," Daniel murmured, his brow furrowing. He guided Rose back into the house, motioning for Frank to join them inside.

"Do you think he's out there, watching?" Rose asked.

"Probably not. He wouldn't want to risk being caught."

And yet he'd risked walking up on her porch in broad daylight and leaving the envelope in front of her door.

Or had it been broad daylight? They'd come in through the back early this morning. The message could have been propped against the door since then. A warning of what he was about to do, or a gloat about what he'd already done?

"Let's get that to the station before we jump to any conclusions," Frank said quietly. "We need to see what's inside. And I have questions for you, too."

Rose glanced at Daniel. He gazed back at her, his expression a mixture of consolation and regret.

"I'll go get dressed," she said.

"No obvious prints or fibers," Frank Carter told Daniel and Rose when he returned to the detectives' office where they'd been waiting for over an hour. "We're running more tests to see if we can pull some prints from the paper, but it's iffy." He handed Rose a sheet of paper. "This is what we found inside."

Rose looked at the photocopy of the notepaper. Centered in the middle were the words, "Sorry about your friend."

Her veins filled with ice water.

"Same paper as last time. Standard word processing instead of block printing this time," Frank continued. "Times New Roman, twelve-point type. No obvious printer inconsistencies, but if we could find the printer we could probably match them up. Our evidence technicians will take a closer look at that, as well."

Daniel placed his hand at the center of Rose's back, his steadying touch welcome. She leaned closer, taking strength from his warmth. "Why has he targeted me?" she asked Frank.

"I'm not sure," Frank admitted. "You were mentioned in the write-up of the neighborhood meeting. Maybe he thinks you're interfering with his business."

Rose wasn't so sure. There seemed to be something personal about his interest, as if he could sense her connection to him.

What would he do if he ever learned that she could foresee his vicious acts?

The phone on Frank's desk rang. He grabbed it. "Carter."

Daniel's hand moved in a gentle circle over Rose's spine, radiating warmth through her shaky limbs. "You holding up?" he murmured for her ears only.

She nodded.

"Okay, will do," Frank said into the phone. He hung up and looked at Daniel. "That was my captain, Sheila Green. She wants to see you in her office to discuss what you can contribute to our investigation."

"Right now?"

Frank nodded. "Down the hall to the right. I'll keep Ms. Browning company while you're in there."

Daniel dropped his hand away from Rose's back and stood, giving her a quick, reassuring look before heading for the exit.

"How are you holding up?" Frank asked Rose, dragging her attention away from Daniel's retreating back.

"I'm okay," she said. "Tired of losing my friends."

Frank nodded, his expression sympathetic. "It's never just the victim who suffers."

He was right. It wasn't. It was family, friends, whole neighborhoods. In the last week, she'd seen security-company vans in front of three different houses in her neighborhood. She was trying to figure out how to pay for an alarm system for her own home.

All because of one man's brutal violence.

"It's convenient you're here," Frank added. "I need to discuss Melissa Bannerman's murder with you."

Rose willed herself not to panic. She had nothing to hide—nothing that could affect the investigation, anyway. She lifted her chin. "I'll help however I can."

"We interviewed Mark Phagan this morning. He said you and Ms. Bannerman had a recent falling out."

Rose's heart flip-flopped. "We had a disagreement and agreed to part company," she admitted carefully.

"A disagreement." Frank's eyes glimmered with a mixture of curiosity, bemusement and doubt.

He knew.

She sighed. "I suppose Mark told you what it was about."

"He did." Frank picked up a scuffed baseball from

his desk and rolled it between his hands, the leather making a dry swishing sound against his palms. He remained silent, watching her through narrowed eyes.

She held her silence, as well, refusing to be intimidated. If he wanted to know about the death veils, he could ask her.

"Does Daniel know about your claims?" Frank asked finally.

The question surprised her. "Yes."

"But he's a scientist."

"I didn't say he believed me," she responded.

Frank's lips curved without quite making it to a smile. "I suppose there are other reasons he might want to stick around."

Rose frowned, not liking his tone, then realized her reaction was exactly what the detective was looking for. She cleared her expression, not willing to give anything more away about her complicated relationship with Daniel.

"I mean, you're his type." Frank cocked his head, his gaze moving over her in a slow sweep that was just short of invasive. "Small, pretty, fragile…"

Rose's only outward reaction was to sit a little straighter, but inside she was growing angry. Fragile? She was a lot of things, but fragile wasn't one of them.

"You kind of look like her, too." Frank's voice softened. His eyes lowered, as if he were lost in memory.

Rose couldn't stop herself from responding. "Her?"

Frank's gaze swung back to hers, fierce and intense. "Tina. My sister. Daniel's fiancée."

Rose held still, though Daniel's response when she'd asked him about being in the market for a wedding flashed through her head. *Almost been there, almost done that.*

"They didn't make it to the altar," Frank added.

Rose bit her tongue to keep from blurting the question the detective obviously wanted her to ask.

"I suppose he's told you about her, though."

"What does this have to do with Melissa?"

Frank set the ball on his desk. His gaze narrowed. "Where were you last night after midnight?"

"Home."

"Alone?"

She pressed her lips together. "Daniel was with me."

He didn't look surprised. "He went looking for Melissa last night after she left him a message. Did you go with him?"

"Yes."

"Even though you and Melissa weren't on good terms."

"I was worried about her."

"Because of the—what did Mr. Phagan say you called it? Death veil?" Frank seemed to take pleasure in her discomfiture, feeding it with his knowing looks and deliberate jabs. Daniel's friend was good at playing bad cop when he wanted to. No doubt it served him well in interrogations.

But she wouldn't play that game. "Yes, because of the death veil," she responded firmly. "I was right to be worried."

"Can't argue with that." Frank's expression softened. "Did Ms. Bannerman ever mention receiving threats, or maybe noticing someone following her around? Did she change her behavior in any way over the past few days that would make you think she was worried about her personal safety?"

Rose shook her head. "She had a security system put in recently, but I think she saw it as a precaution, not a reaction to any specific threats against her."

"Do you know what company?"

"Mark can probably tell you more. Oh, wait," she added, remembering the card that the security technician had given her at the neighborhood meeting. She found the card in her purse and handed it to him. "The installer was Jesse Phillips, with Professional Security Services. Melissa introduced us. She thought I might be interested in a security system of my own."

Frank looked at the card, his brow creasing. He jotted down the information from the card before handing it back to her. "Did you know Alice Donovan also had a Professional Security Systems alarm system at her apartment?"

"I think Alice referred them to Melissa." Uneasiness settled in the pit of Rose's stomach. Had Jesse Phillips installed Alice Donovan's system, as well?

She could still remember the way he'd looked at her at the neighborhood meeting, his gaze wandering, taking in her breasts and legs. He hadn't really tried to hide his interest, had he?

Had he been toying with her, even then? He could have found out where she lived easily enough. No big effort from there to leave a cryptic note thanking her for setting up the neighborhood meeting—or giving her his condolences for a death he'd caused.

Was it possible?

She told Frank about meeting Jesse Phillips at the

neighborhood meeting. "It could be a coincidence, but—"

"But you received the first note the next day," Frank finished with a nod. "We'll look into it."

Rose glanced toward the doorway, wishing Daniel would come back. She wanted to see if he thought her theory was plausible.

It could be the break in the case they'd been hoping for.

CAPTAIN SHEILA GREEN was a tall, thin woman who was probably in her early fifties but looked at least a decade younger. Her café-au-lait skin was wrinkle-free and unblemished, her short black Afro only lightly flecked with gray. She greeted Daniel with a brief smile and waved him into the chair in front of her desk. "Pleased to meet you, Dr. Hartman. I've followed your work for years."

"Thank you. Appreciate your meeting with me."

She steepled her hands in front of her, looking at him over the top of her half-glasses. "How did you learn of this case?"

"I've been tracking murder cases all over the Midwest and southeast that feature certain similarities," Daniel answered. He outlined the work he'd been doing for the past few years since leaving the FBI for the private sector. "I believe this man has killed over twenty women in the past seven years. Perhaps, more, since I can't be sure I've discovered them all."

Captain Green's eyes narrowed slightly. She pushed a button on her phone. "Sharon? Has Agent Brody arrived yet?"

Brody? Daniel's muscles bunched.

The secretary answered an affirmative.

Captain Green's smile looked distinctly predatory. "Please send him in."

A moment later the office door opened and Special Agent Cal Brody of the FBI swaggered in, meeting Daniel's stony gaze with a grin. "Hello, Doc. Long time, no see."

Not long enough, Daniel thought. "Thought you retired."

Brody laughed. "I hear you want in on this case. We've already got a profiler from Quantico working on it."

"Two pairs of eyes are better than one."

Brody dropped into the empty chair next to Daniel and laid a thick file folder on the edge of the desk in front of him. He turned a bright smile toward Captain Green. "Hi, Sheila. Thanks for calling me in on this meeting."

Daniel glanced at the captain. A slight smile curved her lips and she lifted one perfectly arched eyebrow.

"I don't have any real objection to your coming in on this thing," Brody continued, calling Daniel's attention back to him. "Like you say, another pair of eyes won't hurt a thing."

"But?"

"But we're a little concerned about your relationship to a material witness in the case."

Rose, of course. "Concerned how?"

"When she first showed up on our radar as a peripheral witness in the investigation of Alice Donovan's murder, the name rang a bell with me." Brody picked up the file folder from the edge of Captain Green's desk and flipped through until he found a sheet of paper. He handed the sheet to Daniel.

It was a photocopy of a newspaper article about a case that had been big news a little over a year ago—a politically motivated kidnapping that had led to murder and a huge scandal. A black-and-white photo of a man and a woman speaking to each other, heads close, took up the right side of the article.

Daniel read the caption. "Lieutenant J. McBride of the Borland Police Department confers with elementary schoolteacher Lily Browning, who allegedly claims to have seen visions of Abby Walters, missing since her mother's murder."

Lily Browning.

Rose's sister.

Chapter Eleven

Brody and the captain looked expectantly at Daniel. He remained silent, preferring to see what direction they were going with the information about Rose's sister.

"You can understand our concerns," Captain Green said when it became clear he had no response.

"Especially considering our conversation this morning with Mark Phagan," Brody added. "Ms. Bannerman recently fired Ms. Browning over some rather interesting claims—"

"I know what the split was about." Daniel tried to ignore the queasy heat churning in the pit of his stomach.

Brody looked surprised. "So you know what she's claiming. And you don't find that…alarming?"

Daniel met the FBI agent's narrowed gaze. "She's not a danger to herself or anyone else."

"You sound like McBride."

Daniel looked at the newspaper photo. McBride looked like television's idea of a typical cop—muscular and solid, with short-cropped hair and strong, craggy features. No-nonsense written all over him. "So McBride listened to Lily Browning?"

"Listened to her? Hell, he married her." Brody slanted Daniel a look. "He didn't seem the gullible type, either."

"Never said I believed her, just that she's not dangerous."

"She says she sees visions of people about to die." Captain Green shook her head. "She's either lying or insane."

Daniel didn't argue. He couldn't defend Rose when he wasn't yet sure what he thought about her claims. "Let's get to the point, okay? Am I in on the case or not?"

Captain Green's eyes narrowed, but she picked up a folder from her desk and handed it to him. "Copies of everything we have on the murders. Crime-scene photos, lab reports, witness interviews, the whole shebang. I'm trusting you with these because of your reputation and on the recommendation of people you've worked with before. And, yes, I did check."

"Of course." Daniel kept his expression neutral, but excitement was already building in the pit of his belly. The information inside the file he held was a gold mine to a profiler. All he needed was one piece of data he didn't already have. One bit of evidence that could make or break the case.

Captain Green's voice grew stern. "If anything in that file shows up in the media without our express permission, there will be dire consequences. Understood?"

"Understood. Thank you, ma'am." Daniel headed for the exit, sparing a look at Agent Brody, who looked dyspeptic. Feds talked a good game about interagency cooperation, but most thought the locals were rubes and outside "experts" were shills.

He suspected Brody's opinion of former FBI profilers wasn't much better. Especially profilers who consorted with the likes of Rose Browning or her flaky sisters.

DANIEL WAS QUIET on the drive back to her house. Rose darted a glance at him. "I think Jesse Phillips is a good lead," she said.

"Probably," he agreed absently.

"Maybe whoever did the background check on him at the security company missed something important."

"Mmm-hmm."

His unresponsiveness was beginning to get on her nerves. "I think Detective Carter was interrogating me."

That earned her a quick glance.

"He knows about the death veils."

"I know." Daniel didn't sound happy about it.

She nibbled her lip. "He asked a lot of questions about my relationship with Melissa." She told him what Frank had asked, about the suspicion he hadn't been able to hide. She considered mentioning the detective's out-of-the-blue comment of his sister, but decided against it. Just because the detective had been fishing for information about her relationship with Daniel didn't mean she was about to do the same. If Daniel wanted to tell her about Tina, he would.

"Once I mentioned Jesse Phillips, he changed his focus," she added. "But he didn't act like he considered Mark Phagan a suspect at all."

"He's not going to share his theories with someone outside the investigative team."

"Y'all will look into it, won't you? I mean, you said

you always try to eliminate the significant other, first, right?"

"We'll find out where he was last night and the night of Alice's murder. Okay?"

"Okay."

The message light was flashing on Rose's answering machine when she let herself and Daniel into the kitchen through the back door. She rewound the tape and listened.

"Rose, this is Sandra Martin. I wanted to confirm our meeting this afternoon to discuss my wedding. 1:00 p.m. at Office Park West, Suite 400. Please call if you can't make it."

Rose looked at her watch. Almost twelve-thirty. She'd forgotten all about the appointment. "I should reschedule."

"Take the meeting." Daniel turned to look at her. "It'll be good to think about something else for a couple of hours."

He was right. Concentrating on business would be a welcome distraction. "What about you?"

He patted the file folder. "I have plenty to do."

She didn't know why she found his eagerness to dig into the file so discomfiting. Of course he wanted to fill in all the blanks. He'd been looking for this killer for years.

But did he have to seem so eager to get rid of her?

She stopped herself there. She'd never been the needy type. She wasn't about to start now. "I'll go change." She jogged upstairs to change into a fresh business suit, stopping only long enough to run a brush through her hair and apply a touch of mascara and lipstick.

Daniel was waiting for her downstairs, the file folder tucked under his arm. "I'll wait in the car."

Rose shook her head. "That's not necessary."

He gave her a pointed look. "You've received two messages from someone who in all probability is a vicious murderer. I don't think it's a good idea for you to go out alone."

He was right. "Okay."

"Let's take your car so I can get a head start on these files." He held the back door open for her. When she paused to lock up, he kept going, reaching the car well ahead of her.

By the time she slid behind the steering wheel, he had the file folder open, his brow furrowed with concentration, while he waited for her to unlock the door.

No doubt single-mindedness had made him the top criminal profiler he was, she thought as she buckled her seat belt. What he was doing was important and necessary.

But coming in second to a stack of crime-scene photos was rough on a girl's ego.

ONCE ROSE DISAPPEARED through the doors of Office Park West, Daniel put down the case file and pulled out his handheld computer. He connected to the Internet and brought up a Web search engine. He punched "Andrew Walters kidnapping" into the small keypad and hit Enter. The search engine listed scores of articles from a variety of online newspapers.

He selected the story on the *Borland Courier* Web site—the local rag would probably have the most in-depth coverage. Scanning the archived article, he jotted down names. Lieutenant J. McBride was listed, along with McBride's captain, Alex Vann, and another detective named Theo Baker.

Daniel needed to know what had happened during the Abby Walters' kidnapping case to convince J. McBride that Lily Browning's "visions" were the real thing. Was it really as simple as the man falling in love with her?

Daniel couldn't buy that. He was halfway gone where Rose was concerned, but the more he felt himself becoming emotionally entangled with her, the more he fought the idea that she might actually be telling the truth about the death veils.

That was a madness he couldn't afford.

He dialed the number, already having decided on his cover story. He asked for Theo Baker, figuring McBride wouldn't talk to a stranger about his sister-in-law.

"Baker."

"Detective, Dan Haley with the *Montgomery Advertiser.* I'm doing a follow-up story on the Walters kidnapping, and I wonder if you could spare a moment to discuss your part in the case."

"I'm a little busy." Baker sounded wary.

"I'm mostly interested in a side story—Lily Browning's involvement in the case."

"Hold a sec." There was a click and then silence.

Interesting.

A moment later there was another click and a gruff voice asked, "You say you're with the *Montgomery Advertiser?*"

"Yes. With whom am I speaking now?"

"Lieutenant McBride."

The husband. Great. "Lieutenant, I'm doing a feature article on the use of psychics in criminal investigations, and I found an article that mentions a woman named Lily Browning who aided your investigation into the kidnapping of Abby Walters."

"You said your name is Dan Haley?"

Time to drop names. "I spoke to an FBI agent named Cal Brody this morning. He mentioned the case."

"Brody." Distaste tinged McBride's voice. "Figures."

"Apparently, Ms. Browning's sister, Rose, is a material witness in a string of murders in Birmingham."

McBride's voice deepened with alarm. "Rose?"

Daniel decided to go for broke. "She claims to be able to foresee the murders."

McBride was silent for a long moment, so silent that Daniel was afraid he'd cut the connection.

"Lieutenant?"

"Foresee them how?" McBride's voice was low and strangled.

He didn't know about the death veils? Even more interesting.

"She calls them death veils." Daniel briefly explained what Rose was claiming to see. When he finished, silence stretched across the phone line, thick and tense.

"I can't help you," McBride said finally. "Sorry."

The line clicked dead.

Daniel put down the handheld computer. So much for tricking a cop for information. As devious ploys went, playing reporter hadn't been the most inspired. But he'd learned one interesting tidbit: Rose's family apparently didn't know about the death veils.

He pushed aside his curiosity and picked up one of the police reports on the first murder. He began reading, making notes of similarities and disparities between the Birmingham murders and the others he'd been investigating over the past few years.

He'd made it through the second murder when his cell phone rang. He glanced at the phone display and found an unfamiliar number. He punched the receive button. "Yeah?"

"There's no Dan Haley at the *Montgomery Advertiser,*" McBride's gravelly voice greeted him. "There is, however, a former FBI profiler and current criminology professor named Daniel Hartman who happens to have this cell-phone number."

Daniel sighed. "Hello, to you, too, Lieutenant."

"I called Cal Brody, too. He wasn't happy to hear you were shooting off your mouth about him and his murder investigation."

"It's my investigation now, too."

"So why didn't you just tell me who you were?"

"Would you have been any more willing to talk about your sister-in-law?"

"No," McBride conceded.

"I mean her no harm," Daniel assured him. "In fact, I consider her a friend. I'm sitting in her car right now."

"Is she there?"

"No, she had a business appointment."

"So, if I call and ask her who Daniel Hartman is and why he's calling me behind her back, you'd be okay with that?"

Daniel sighed. "I'd rather you not do that."

"Thought not." A hint of smug satisfaction tinged

McBride's voice. "So, if you're Rose's friend, as you say, why not just ask *her* whatever it is you want to know?"

"At least, she's told *me* about the death veils," Daniel countered. "You don't seem to know anything about them."

"How long has she been seeing them?"

"I assumed it was something she thinks she's been able to do since childhood."

"'She thinks,'" McBride repeated Daniel's phrasing.

"I'm…unconvinced."

McBride made a soft huffing sound that might have been a half chuckle. "Know the feeling."

"You must have changed your mind at some point," Daniel murmured. "After all, you married your psychic."

McBride's voice dropped an octave. "That's none of your business."

"Frankly, I'm more interested in why Rose has never told you or your wife about the death veils."

"So am I," McBride admitted. "Is she okay?"

Daniel cocked his head, surprised by the concern evident in the cop's voice. Until this point, he'd shown nothing but surly antagonism. "She's tougher than she looks."

"How many murders are we talking about?"

"Four, so far. Here in Birmingham, at least."

McBride's voice darkened. "Serial murders?"

"Yeah."

"Is Rose in danger?"

"Not immediate danger," Daniel answered carefully. He didn't have the right to share sensitive information about the investigation with someone outside the Birmingham Police Department, even with another lawman.

"Why did you call Theo Baker instead of me?" McBride asked.

"I thought he'd be more likely to be open about your wife's involvement in the Walters kidnapping case." Checking his watch, Daniel looked across the parking lot at the glass-fronted entrance of the office building. Rose had been inside for thirty minutes. She'd probably be on her way out soon.

"You're right about one thing," McBride said after a short pause, "these death veils are news to me."

"So they're not something she's had all her life."

"No, they're not."

Daniel frowned, remembering his conversation with the Willow Grove mayor soon after he'd met Rose. The mayor had implied that Rose and her sisters were well known in the community for their odd ways. Of course, if one sister claimed to be a psychic, maybe the whole family was tainted by it. "So I take it you thought your wife was the only one of her sisters with any sort of... unusual ability?"

"Why do you want to know?"

"It's not a hard question to answer, Lieutenant."

"All three of them have...unusual abilities," McBride answered, his voice tight.

"But seeing death veils isn't one of them?"

"Rose used to see something else. But she lost that ability a few months ago."

"Around Christmas?" Daniel asked, reminded of what the Willow Grove mayor had told him about the murder-suicide Rose had witnessed.

McBride hesitated.

"I know about Carrie and Dillon Granville," Daniel added, hoping to spur the detective into filling in the rest of the blanks. "I know Rose planned their wedding and I know that she walked in on Dillon right after he'd killed his wife. I know she saw him commit suicide."

"That's when it happened," McBride conceded.

"When she lost her other gift."

"Understandable, I guess," McBride murmured. "The true-love veils had brought those two together. Seeing them ripped apart in such a violent, horrible way—"

"True-love veils?"

As he listened to McBride explain the concept of true-love veils in a flat, expressionless voice, Daniel's stomach settled into a hot, queasy knot beneath his rib cage. It explained so much that had puzzled him about Rose—the sense he got from time to time that she had once been a very different woman.

Maybe it even explained the searching gaze she'd given him that morning as she'd taken him into her arms. Had she been looking for a true-love veil, some evidence that what they were about to do was more significant than just using sex to temporarily escape the looming specter of death?

"Are you still there?" McBride's voice buzzed in his ear.

"Yeah, I'm here."

"I'm not going to try to convince you to believe what Rose is saying," McBride said. "I wouldn't have listened in your place. But I'll tell you this. I saw Lily's visions come true in ways I can't explain. And even then, I almost didn't listen to her. It would have cost me my daughter if I hadn't. So be skeptical all you want. Convince yourself that she can't possibly be right. But don't ignore her."

The hairs on the back of Daniel's neck prickled.

"If she tells you something is going to happen, check it out," McBride continued, his voice softening. "If she's wrong, you've chased your tail for an hour or two. Big deal—you do that in any investigation. But if she's right, you just might save a life." McBride hung up without saying goodbye.

Daniel closed his phone and laid his head back against the headrest, shutting his eyes. McBride's words rang in his head. *Don't ignore her.*

Daniel released a slow breath, shaking his head. No worry there. He couldn't ignore Rose Browning if he tried.

IF ANYTHING, Daniel was even more preoccupied when Rose returned to the car. He answered her attempts at small talk with flat, one-word responses, his gaze glued to the folder in his lap. Rose fell silent for the rest of the drive.

The meeting with Sandra Martin had gone well, a much-needed distraction from the past few tragic days. For a few minutes, Rose had almost felt the old excitement that had always made being a wedding planner the most enjoyable job in the world.

So much had changed that day in Bridey Woods.

Daniel followed her into the house and took a cursory look around before returning to the kitchen. "I'm going to my motel room to grab my things. Not a good idea, your living alone here while Orion is sending you messages."

She licked her lips, the memory of his body, hard and hot against hers, sending heat flooding into her belly again. She tried to read his intentions in his shuttered expression. Was moving in here about more than keeping her safe?

"If you don't have a spare room set up, I'll make do with the sofa," he added.

She crossed to the refrigerator and opened it, chiding herself for feeling disappointed. "I'll put some clean sheets on the spare bed. You want something to eat before you go?"

He shook his head. "I'll pick up something on the way back. Unless you're too hungry to wait."

Though she hadn't eaten all day, the thought of food made her queasy. She closed the refrigerator door. "I can wait."

"Chinese okay?"

"That's fine. I like shrimp in lobster sauce." She reached for her purse, but he closed his hand over hers.

"My treat."

Beneath his fingers, her flesh tingled. Amazing how much one simple touch from him could affect her.

He let go of her hand. "When I get back, we need to talk about a few things," he murmured.

She lifted her gaze, unnerved by the serious tone of his voice. His eyes locked with hers, his expression searching, as if she were a mystery to be solved.

Maybe she was. She didn't understand herself these days; she could hardly expect it of Daniel.

"Lock the doors behind me and don't let anyone in till I get back." He headed for the back door.

She locked up behind him, parting the pale blue curtains covering the window in the back door to watch him stride up the slope to where his Jeep was parked in the alley. She didn't let the curtains fall until he was out of sight.

With Daniel gone, silence surrounded her, looming and oppressive, broken only by the faint rumble of thunder in the distance. Dark clouds were rolling in from the west, promising a rainy night. With an old house like hers, there was a fifty-fifty chance the power would go out. That meant candles.

Candles and Daniel. A dangerous combination.

Restless, she went to the living room and put a CD in the player, turning the volume up until Patty Loveless's raw alto bounced off the walls, driving the quiet into the recesses of the old house. By the third song, she was singing along, the music bleeding from her taut nerves. She pushed herself off the sofa and moved to the beat of the twangy waltz, tension flowing out of her as she twirled and swayed.

When her doorbell rang, the discordant noise scraped along the nerves of her spine, jerking her out of rhythm. She turned down the player and crept to the front door. Heart pounding, she peered through the fish-eye lens.

Her sister, Lily, stood on the porch.

Shaky with relief, Rose unlocked the door, barely resisting the urge to throw herself into her sister's arms.

But the grim look on Lily's face cut her relief short.
"What's wrong?"

Lily's lower lip trembled. "When were you going to
tell me about the death veils?"

Chapter Twelve

Daniel checked his e-mail before packing up his laptop. There were a handful of official university e-mails and a couple from his assistant, Steve.

"Did a search for Rose Browning," the e-mail read. "Found some blogs out of her neck of the woods that mention her. Fascinating stuff. Quite a rep as a matchmaker. Hints of some mystical mojo. Can I meet her? Pretty please?"

Mystical mojo, indeed.

What he'd learned from Rose's brother-in-law only complicated his mixed-up feelings about her. Even as she wriggled deeper under his skin, he kept discovering more reasons why letting her get any closer was nothing short of insanity.

He was a scientist. He dealt in facts, in the tangible. People in law enforcement sometimes talked about what profilers did as voodoo or magic, but he knew it was all about logic and patterns of behavior. Killers weren't nearly as complicated as people wanted to believe. They killed out of anger or greed or jealousy, and even the superstars of the murder world, the serial killers, had knowable reasons for their murders.

If he found Orion, it wasn't going to be the result of psychic messages. Of that, he was positive.

At the same time, he considered as he packed his car for the trip back to Rose's, was it fair to dismiss what she had to say? She had two sisters who claimed to have some sort of psychic gift. Obviously, they'd lived in a household where magic was considered a viable explanation for actions and behaviors. Maybe Rose was using terms like *true-love veils* and *death veils* to describe her native instinct for reading people.

After all, what if he'd been raised to believe in the supernatural? Might he use mystical terms like *mind reading* to describe his ability to predict and explain criminal behavior?

Perhaps, what Rose ascribed to magic was nothing more than a keen understanding of human nature. An uncanny ability to recognize compatibility between sexually attracted couples. And maybe she'd seen in Orion's victims some sort of increased probability of actions that would put them in jeopardy.

Alice Donovan had been at the bar the night she'd died, to drink and dance away the memory of a bad romantic breakup. She might have been more reckless than usual with her personal safety—something Rose would have picked up on. And Melissa's blindness to betrayal, such as that of her cheating fiancé, might have made her more vulnerable to becoming the killer's victim.

Rose wasn't a liar and she wasn't insane. Daniel

knew that on the gut level. So what, if his new theory didn't explain everything perfectly? It came close.

Maybe he could live with that.

"I CAN'T BELIEVE he called McBride." Rose looked at her sister with dismay.

"McBride didn't know what to think." Lily touched her sister's arm. "He's heard of the man, of course, but you know he's protective of the Browning girls. He didn't like what Daniel seemed to be insinuating about you."

Rose could imagine. "Daniel doesn't believe me."

"But you predicted four murders." Lily looked indignant.

"Would that have been enough for McBride, at first?"

Lily sighed. "You know the answer."

Rose pulled back the window curtain beside her, gazing out at the gathering storm clouds. "At least he's still listening to me. Or was, until Agent Brody got hold of him."

"I can't believe Brody used me against you." Lily scowled.

"I doubt Daniel put up much resistance." Rose let the curtain drop, tears burning her throat.

"Is there something going on between you two?"

Rose looked away, reliving the feel of Daniel's mouth against her throat. "No."

At least, not what she'd hoped.

Lily seemed to accept her answer. "I wish you'd told me about this when you first started seeing the death veils."

The tears welling in Rose's eyes spilled down her cheeks. "I thought they were punishment for getting things so wrong with Dillon and Carrie. I was ashamed."

Lily bent forward. "You can't blame yourself for that."

Rose fought the urge to cry on her sister's shoulder. "I don't want to see death anymore."

Lily stroked her hair. "I spent years running from my visions, so I don't have the right to lecture. But you can't keep torturing yourself." She dropped her hand. "Does Iris know?"

Rose nodded.

Lily's eyes dropped, but not soon enough to hide the hurt in their golden depths.

Rose touched Lily's hand. "I told Iris only a couple of days ago, and only because she wouldn't leave till I confessed."

Lily's lips quirked. "Sounds like her."

"I was going to call you this weekend to see if I could come visit, but everything…fell apart." An unexpected ache bloomed in Rose's chest.

"I'm so sorry about your friend. Last night must have been hell. Have you even had any sleep yet?"

"A little." Rose glanced at the kitchen clock. "Lily, it's almost three. Who's picking up Casey from school?"

"McBride. I'm yours for the night if you need me."

"I'm fine. Your daughter needs you at home."

Emotion flickered in Lily's eyes. "My daughter."

Rose smiled. "Still going well?"

Lily nodded. "She goes to a therapist a couple of times

a month, to make sure she's adjusting, but I swear, she has everything worked out in her head already. It's amazing, considering what her life was like after the abduction."

"Poor Mrs. Grainger," Rose murmured, thinking of the disturbed woman who'd kidnapped Casey when the child was only three. "Losing her own child and then losing her mind."

"She was Casey's mother for six years. No matter how sick she was, she must have done a few things right for Casey to have been able to adjust so well. Casey still misses her."

Tears prickled in Rose's eyes. "Poor baby."

"I think it helps that she and Abby Walters are going to the same school now. Casey still takes Abby under her wing. I think it makes her feel in control."

Rose sighed. In control—she'd felt that way once. It was time to feel in control again. She'd call security companies first thing in the morning to see about getting an alarm system installed. She'd just have to pinch pennies to afford it.

Thinking of alarm systems reminded her of Jesse Phillips and the discussion she'd had with Frank Carter that morning. She doubted the police had checked his alibis for the nights in question yet. They were probably still tracking down Mark Phagan's movements from the night before.

She was tired of feeling helpless, afraid to venture from her own house alone for fear of becoming a victim, thanks to the mysterious messages she'd received. If she stayed at home all the time, she couldn't even use the one tool at her disposal: The death veils that, at least, gave her fair warning of who the killer would next strike. She couldn't live like this.

There had to be something she could do besides hide.

Lily leaned toward her. "If you need me to stay with you, I really do think Casey'll be okay with her daddy for one night."

"I'll be fine." She looked up at her sister. "But before you go, I could use your help with something."

DANIEL SPENT THE DRIVE from the Chinese restaurant to Rose's house on the phone with his assistant, going over the research he wanted Steve to do for him over the weekend. "I need as much background as you can find on Mark Allen Phagan, born in Tuscaloosa, Alabama, and currently a lawyer in Birmingham, Alabama, and a man in his early thirties named Jesse Phillips," he said as he pulled into the alley behind Rose's house. "Only info I have on Phillips is a current place of employment—Professional Security Systems in Birmingham."

"Got it," Steve said. "Anything else?"

Daniel stared at the empty parking spot where Rose's Chevrolet had been earlier that afternoon. "That's it, for now." He rang off quickly, tucking the phone in his breast pocket.

Parking, he grabbed the bag of Chinese food and walked around the house, hoping Rose's car was there.

But the car in the driveway wasn't hers.

Tamping down his rising alarm, he tried the doorbell. No answer. He knocked on the door hard enough to sting his knuckles. "Rose?"

Still no reply.

The back door was locked, as well. He pulled out his phone to call her cell phone and noticed the voice mail message indicator. He retrieved the message and found himself listening to Rose Browning's terse voice.

"Daniel, it's Rose. I've changed my mind. You can't stay here. I'm heading out on an errand, but I'll be home by five at the latest if you want to call."

His heart thumped against his ribs. An errand? Was she insane? He dialed her cell-phone number. Her voice-mail message picked up immediately.

Damn it!

Anxiety overtook anger as he waited for the beep. "Rose, it's Daniel. What's going on? Call when you get this message."

He ended the call and leaned against the door frame, his pulse racing. What if she'd made the call under duress? Her voice had sounded odd. Strained and tight.

He pressed his forehead against the door, muttering a low curse—at himself for not taking her with him to the motel, at her for leaving the house when he'd told her to stay put.

Tamping down his rising fear, he sank onto the wrought iron bench by the back door and tried to figure out what to do next.

ROSE PULLED INTO a parking space in front of a squat brick-and-steel storefront on Seventh Avenue. The sign on the front wall read, Professional Security Systems.

"Doesn't your prime suspect work here?" Lily asked.

Rose nodded.

"Have you lost your mind?"

"I can't sit around and wait to read about the next

victim." Rose unbuckled her seat belt and opened the car door.

Lily met her on the sidewalk. "How is coming here supposed to help?"

"If Jesse Phillips is the killer, then odds are, he's at least considering killing some of the women he works with. If so, I'll see a death veil and I'll know who the next victim is."

"And do what? Warn her?" Lily shot Rose a pointed look.

"I'll figure it out as I go."

"That's a recipe for disaster," Lily warned.

"What's the worst that can happen?" Rose countered. "I get a brochure on their services and I go home. No harm done." Rose didn't feel quite as sanguine as she sounded, but she preferred action to inertia, and taking a look around Jesse Phillips' workplace seemed relatively safe. She pushed through the front door and stopped short.

Covering the face of the receptionist was a shimmering death veil.

"Do you see something?" Lily whispered.

Rose nodded.

Another woman stepped into the reception area, carrying a slim stack of file folders. A death veil flickered over her features, as well.

"Ms. Browning?"

A man's voice close by jarred her nerves. She jerked toward the sound, trying to hide her growing alarm.

Jesse Phillips stood a few feet away, his gaze fixed on her. A tremor rattled through her, and she took a defensive step back before she registered the fact that

Jesse wasn't alone. Frank Carter stood to his right, gripping Jesse's upper arm in his tight grip. A second man, obviously another detective, gripped his other arm.

Rose cleared her throat. "Detective Carter."

Frank released Jesse's arm and stepped closer. His voice was low and intense. "You're seeing something."

Rose glanced at her sister. A faint death veil shimmered over her features, as well. Rose's stomach clenched into a knot.

"What is it?" Lily asked, touching Rose's arm.

"Every woman here is wearing a death veil," Rose murmured. "Including you."

Lily's eyes widened with alarm.

Rose pulled a powder compact from her purse. Holding her breath, she checked her reflection in the mirror.

It was there. Fainter than the others, but unmistakable.

She looked up and saw four sets of eyes staring at her. She focused on Jesse Phillips, trying to read his expression. Another shudder moved through her, making her hand shake.

She slapped the compact closed. "Let's get out of here."

Frank caught her elbow as she started toward the door. "You see more than one at a time?"

"Not usually," she admitted. "I did at the neighborhood meeting. And now. The last time, they faded away."

"How do you explain it?" Frank asked, his brow furrowed.

The other detective and Jesse Phillips moved past them, heading out the door. Rose waited before answering Frank. "I don't know. Maybe he gets excited after a kill. Can't decide who's next, so he imagines killing them all." Rose jerked her elbow from Frank's grasp and fled outside. She filled her burning lungs with cool October air.

Lily caught up with her. "Rose?"

Rose closed her eyes, afraid to look at her sister. Please let it fade, she thought.

"Look at me." Lily's voice shook.

Rose opened her eyes. Lily's face was clear. She almost wilted. "It's gone."

Lily released a huff of breath.

Frank approached, brow furrowed. "You still see anything?"

Rose glanced at her car window. Her reflection stared back, now free of the death veil. "No. All clear now."

Frank nodded slowly, his expression still troubled. "We have to take Phillips in for questioning. Are you sure you're going to be okay getting home?"

"I'll be fine," Rose assured him. She nodded toward Phillips, who gazed at them, a scowl on his face, as the other detective nudged him into the backseat of the sedan. "You think he's a viable suspect?"

"There are things in his background we want to clear up." Frank's expression was guarded. "If I have more questions for you, I'll be in touch." He turned and walked toward the sedan.

"Are you sure you're okay to drive?" Lily asked as they got in the car. "You still look a little shaken."

Rose waved off Lily's concern. "I'm good, really. The death veils must mean Jesse's the killer, don't you think?"

"Could be," Lily agreed.

Rose pulled up the alley behind her house. "Maybe they'll get a search warrant for his house and they'll find something."

"You think he kills them at his own house?"

"He must kill them somewhere—Daniel says nobody's found a murder scene yet, just the dump sites."

As if her mention of Daniel conjured him up, she spotted his Jeep parked where her car normally sat. And the man himself sat on the wrought iron bench on her back patio, a large plastic bag lying on the concrete next to him.

Rose sighed and shut off the car. "Great."

"Daniel, I presume?" Lily murmured.

"I told him not to come."

"Well, he didn't get the message." Lily opened her door.

Daniel stood as they approached. "Didn't get your message until I was already here."

"I'm sorry you had to come all this way."

His eyes narrowed slightly before he turned to Lily and gave a nod. "Daniel Hartman. You must be one of the sisters."

Lily smiled. "Lily. You spoke to my husband earlier."

Daniel's expression shifted as he put the pieces together. "Should have known he'd rat me out."

"What did you expect?" Rose asked.

"A little slack wouldn't have hurt," he replied.

Rose ignored his response and unlocked the back door.

"Since I'm already here, can I put dinner in the refrigerator before it goes bad?" Daniel asked.

Rose waved at the refrigerator, slapped her cell phone down on the counter and headed out of the kitchen.

Lily followed her to the living room. "Brr. That's one cold shoulder you're sporting there."

"You think I'm being harsh?"

Lily shrugged. "Not for me to say."

Daniel joined them a moment later, his expression neutral. Rose couldn't tell if he even gave a damn. "I think the food should be okay. Your sister can have my part."

"Actually," Lily said, "I'd better head home."

Rose forced herself not to coax her sister to stay longer. Lily had better things to do than to play referee. She walked Lily to the front door. "Be careful driving home."

"Lock your doors," Daniel added gruffly.

Rose slanted a look at him. His expression was serious.

"I will," Lily assured him. She squeezed Rose's hand and headed down the porch steps to her car.

Rose watched her until she was on the road. As she stepped back to close the door, she came up flush against Daniel's body.

"Do you have any idea what I thought when I got here and found you gone?" he rasped, his voice low and barely controlled. The smell of him—masculine, feral—filled her lungs as she took a shaky breath. "You want to punish me, find a different way."

She whirled to face him. He was impossibly close, his stormy eyes blazing with emotions, most of them volatile and dark. "You think I was trying to punish you?"

His expression hardened. "Weren't you?"

"I was following a lead of my own."

His eyes narrowed. "You're a detective now?"

She took a step back and ended up flattened against the door. "You expect me to sit home and play damsel in distress?"

"I expect you to do whatever's necessary to stay alive." He pushed forward, trapping her against the door. "A killer is sending you messages. You fit the profile of his victims."

The memory of the faint death veil over her reflection set off a low tremor in her knees. "I know that."

He caught her shoulders in his hands, his fingers digging into her flesh. "Then, act like it!"

She jerked her chin up. "If you wanted to know something about me and my sisters, why didn't you just ask? Did you think I'd lie to you?"

His lips trembled apart with a shaky breath, his gaze flickering down to her mouth. Silence descended, heavy with unspoken words. A tight ache settled in the middle of Rose's chest, trapping her breath.

He moved closer. The air heated between them, thick with tension. "Why didn't you tell me about the true-love veils?"

She fought to breathe, surprised by how much it hurt to hear him speak of her lost gift in tones of such obvious skepticism. She licked her lips. "They're gone now. What difference would it make?"

"Maybe they'd have helped me understand you better."

She clenched her jaw. "And maybe knowing about Tina would have made me understand you a little better."

He jerked back, his eyes narrowing to slits. "Tina?"

His reaction surprised her. "Your former fiancée?"

His chest rose and fell rapidly before he lifted his gaze to meet hers. "Who told you about Tina?"

"Detective Carter."

Daniel's mouth tightened to a thin line.

"He told me you were once engaged to his sister." Rose dropped her gaze. "He said I look like her."

Daniel wrapped his hand around the back of her neck and pulled her toward him. "He's wrong," he said, and slanted his mouth over hers.

Her head spinning from the unexpected assault on her senses, she dug her fingers into his shoulders just to stay upright as his tongue found hers, demanding a response. There was little gentleness in his touch, only hunger and fiery need.

"You're nothing like her," he murmured against her mouth, his hand sliding over her breast, blazing a trail of fire.

A twisting sensation curled through her chest. "Daniel—"

He nipped at her jaw. "Where'd you go this afternoon?"

She slid her hand under his jacket, plucking at his shirt. "Don't change the subject."

"No, tell me. What was so important that you couldn't wait for me to return?" He ran his tongue over the curve of her collarbone, sparking little explosions in the base of her spine.

"I went to the security company where Jesse Phillips works."

Daniel stepped back and gazed down at her. "What?"

She shook her head, not wanting him to stop.

"Daniel, please—" She pulled his head down and kissed him.

For a moment, he returned the kiss, his lips pliant against hers. But too soon he put his hands on her shoulders and held her away. "Why, in hell, would you go there by yourself?"

Rose stepped away from him, needing distance if she was going to be able to hold up her end of what was obviously turning into an interrogation. She couldn't think with him so close, the heat of his body swamping her with need.

She crossed to the archway into the living room, leaning against the wall. "I wasn't by myself. I was with my sister."

"Yeah, she's got bodyguard written all over her." He shook his head. "What if Phillips is the killer?"

"I think he is." She told him about the visit to the security company, leaving out nothing.

His gaze darkened. "You saw a death veil on yourself?"

"On Lily, too." The memory sent ice through her veins. "But they went away."

He shook his head, retreating to the wall.

"They went away," Rose repeated, taking a step toward him.

He looked at her, bleak humor in his eyes. "That would mean more if I believed in them."

She caught his hand, surprised to find it shaking. "Daniel, what is it?"

"You want to know why I didn't marry Tina?" His voice came out like sandpaper.

She nodded, her breath freezing in her chest.

He held her gaze, his eyes searching hers. "Three days before the wedding, I told her I didn't want to get married."

Rose released a soft hiss of breath, caught flat-footed by such a mundane answer. "I see."

He shook his head. "No, you don't. It was the night of my bachelor party. I had a lot to drink as it was, and there were some women at the bar…"

Rose shook her head, not wanting to hear any more. She took a couple of steps sideways, moving away.

Daniel caught her arm. "My friends thought I should sow my last oats. I told them I couldn't. I was about to get married." He exhaled, his shoulders beginning to slump. "They ragged on me. Said I was already henpecked."

Men, Rose thought, not charitably.

"It made me angry. I felt…trapped." His lips curved in a humorless smile. "Cold feet."

"So you gave in to temptation?"

He shook his head. "No."

"Because you loved Tina?"

He turned his gaze to her, his brow creasing as if nobody had thought to ask that question before. "I guess, I did, on some level, or I'd never have asked her to marry me. But I didn't love her enough to make it last. That's what I realized that night. So I went to talk to her."

Rose closed her eyes, filled with pity for Tina. "She must have been crushed."

"That was the odd thing," he said softly. "She wasn't so much hurt as furious. I think that was the moment when I knew, for sure, I was right to break it off."

"Because she was angry?" Rose stiffened with indignation for the girl. "Don't you think she had a right?"

"Of course," Daniel answered. "But her anger was about the wedding, not the engagement. She wanted her big, beautiful fairy-tale wedding and I was screwing it all up."

Rose couldn't believe that was the girl's only concern. "Maybe that's what she said at the time, but I'm sure—"

"I'm not," Daniel said. "I'm not sure she loved me nearly as much as she loved the idea of being married. I've wondered about that for thirteen years."

"Why didn't you just ask her about it later?"

He turned slowly to meet her gaze. "Because when she ran away from me that night, it was the last time I ever saw her alive."

Chapter Thirteen

A chill rippled over Daniel as he waited for Rose's reaction. The day was quickly waning, purple shadows creeping across the floor of Rose's foyer. Her dark eyes glittered in the dimming light, wide and liquid with a chaos of emotions.

"She's dead?" Her voice sounded fragile.

He forced the word out. "Yes."

"How?"

"She was murdered. Her face was carved up and her throat slit."

Rose's gaze fell. She released a slow, shaky breath.

"They found her the next morning in a nearby park. It wasn't far from here, actually. Just off University Boulevard." He watched her carefully, waiting for her to put it together.

"Orion," she whispered.

"That's what I want to find out."

She looked at him. "You must've been the prime suspect."

He could let her think that. It would have been the obvious suspicion, that the fiancé who jilted her the night before she died might have tried to end the engagement in the most permanent way possible. He could nod and skim over that aspect of what happened, and Rose would never know. After all, nobody else knew what he'd done that night.

But the sympathy in her eyes was more than he could bear.

"I might have been, if anyone had known about the breakup," he said. He pressed his lips together, watching the slow metamorphosis of her expression from pity to confusion to horrified realization.

"You didn't tell anyone?"

He closed his eyes. "She'd run away, into the night. I'd thought she was going to a friend's house down the street. I'd let her go, relieved the confrontation was over. I'd gotten in my car and drove home."

"So nobody knew she was gone." Her voice was faint.

"She'd had a room at the back of the house. There had been a wraparound porch there where we'd meet at night after her mother had gone to bed. I'd knock on the window. She'd climb out to meet me." The sudden sweetness of the memory caught him by surprise. There had been good times. He'd let himself forget them. "That's what I'd done that night, so nobody else had known I'd been there. When she'd run away, I'd thought about knocking on the front door to let her mother know, but—" He stopped short, ashamed of his motives.

"You didn't want to face her and explain everything."

"That was my usual M.O. in those days," he admitted, remorse burning a hole in his gut. "Taking the easy way out. Danny Hartman, dragging everyone else into trouble while he slid out of the noose with a smile and a smooth explanation. Keeping quiet seemed… easier. So that's what I did then."

Rose leaned heavily against the wall. "And they had had no idea at all—"

"Until she showed up in the park the next morning."

Rose's eyes closed again. She looked ill.

"I knew, I should've told, but her mother had been a mess. She'd leaned on me a lot. Said she'd thought of me as her son." He shook his head. "I was an extension of Tina to her. I was what she'd felt she had left of her daughter, and I couldn't take that away from her by telling her what had really happened that night."

"But it could have affected the police investigation."

"It wouldn't have." He sank against the wall opposite Rose. "Of course, I can't claim I knew that at the time. I'd let myself get caught up in the lie and, after a certain point, when guilt began to get the best of me, I was trapped. I couldn't change the official history of Tina Carter and Daniel Hartman. Too much had already been built on that foundation. The truth would have hurt a lot of people."

"Including you."

He hated the disappointment in her voice. "Don't worry. I didn't get away unscathed."

"I guess, it explains your obsession with Orion."

"I just want to know if he's the one who killed her."

"What if he's not?"

Daniel didn't know. He hadn't thought that far ahead.

Rose rubbed her temples as if she had a headache. She looked tired, and he remembered that neither of them had had much sleep in the last couple of days. They were in no condition to have this conversation.

He pushed himself away from the wall. "You need food and sleep, in that order."

She started to demur, but he took her arm and turned her toward the kitchen. "It'll take a minute to heat up dinner. We can talk in the morning after we've both had some sleep."

He got the take-out from the refrigerator and spooned the food onto a pair of plates. While Rose sank into a chair at the kitchen table, watching him with her chin resting on her hand, he filled a couple of glasses with iced tea and finished heating the food.

"Why did you tell me?" Rose asked as he pulled the second plate from the microwave oven. He didn't need her to clarify; he knew what she was asking.

He picked up the drinks and put them on the table, looking down into her curious eyes. "Because I needed to."

Her gaze softened. "And I was in the right place at the right time?"

He tucked a loose strand of hair behind her ear. "You were the right person at the right time."

She caught his hand, threading her fingers through his briefly before letting go. She turned her head toward the window, her profile outlined in tangerine light from the dying sun. "Detective Carter didn't even let on that Tina was dead."

"Frank has…issues about Tina," he said, wondering how much of his old friend's secrets he should reveal.

"It can't have been easy to lose his sister so young."

"There was more." Daniel sighed, realizing he needed to talk about the past more than he knew. "Tina was his mother's favorite. She didn't even try to hide it. When Tina died, it was like she'd lost her only child."

"Poor Frank."

"Mary Frances made a shrine of her daughter's room. Kept it immaculate. All her old clothes pressed and hung in the closet. All her stuffed animals and cheerleading trophies lined up where she'd left them. Frank hated that room. Couldn't bring himself to go in there. Kept expecting to see Tina's ghost, sitting on her bed like always. And then he'd know he was the ghost. The kid nobody remembered."

Rose shook her head. "That's horrible. Does her mother still keep the room the same?"

"Mary Frances died earlier this year. That's why Frank moved back to Birmingham."

"He's living there in his old home?"

"Until he gets it ready to sell."

Rose ran her finger over the rim of her glass. "Well, if Jesse Phillips is Orion, you and Frank may know the truth about what happened to Tina sooner than you think. And then maybe he can find some peace."

A flutter of apprehension tightened Daniel's gut. She was right. If Jesse Phillips had killed Melissa and Alice and the other women who'd died here in Birmingham, he could be the man Daniel had spent the last few years of his life trying to find. The long search for justice— for redemption—could be over.

Then what?

He tabled the unnerving question and retrieved the warm plates of food. He grabbed a couple of forks from the drawer by the sink and carried everything to the table, setting the shrimp dish in front of Rose. "Eat."

She picked up the fork and pushed the shrimp around the plate. "Daniel, if you don't believe I'm seeing death veils, what's the alternative? I've been right about four murders—how do you explain that?"

He put down the fork he'd just picked up and looked across the table at her. "How long have you seen veils?"

Her brow wrinkled. "I think I was five or six when I saw the first true-love veil." Her lips curved. "On my parents. I didn't know what it was then, of course. I just remember seeing it made me feel safe."

"That early," he murmured, surprised. He'd figured she'd been older, maybe entering her teens. Five years old was pretty early to have that sort of facility for understanding human behavioral cues.

Then again, a child with parents who loved each other might know, instinctively, that their being together was something right and special. He'd known it about his own parents, hadn't he? Felt, from a young age, that they were more than just two people who loved him. They'd been a unit. A team. When his father had died six years ago, his mother had turned into someone he didn't know anymore, a half person who had to learn how to be whole all over again.

And he'd done nothing to help her, choosing to deal with his own loss by running. Just as he always had.

Guilt stabbed him low in his chest.

"I figured out what the true-love veils were later, when I discovered boys," Rose added, a smile in her voice if not on her lips. "I dispensed boyfriend advice to my older sister Lily and her friends. I was always right. It freaked some of them out—most of them. Lily got so mad at me for driving away her friends with my weirdness."

"I thought she had some weirdness of her own."

"She did." Rose stabbed a shrimp and held it up in front of her, studying its plump curve. "But, by then, she was hiding it. Hiding from it, I guess I should say."

"So you gave good advice to the lovelorn."

"Uncannily good," she said, her voice dry. She put the fork back on her plate, the shrimp still impaled. "Sometimes people didn't want to hear that they were making a mistake."

"How did it work?"

"The veils?"

He nodded.

Her brow crinkled with thought. "I just…saw them. One person's face superimposed over another person's face."

"The faces of soul mates."

The crinkle in her brow deepened. "I always thought so."

"Until the Granvilles."

Her gaze darted up to meet his. "McBride told you about that?"

"No. I learned about that from the mayor of Willow Grove."

A look of dismay flitted over her face. "You called the mayor to check up on me, too?"

"Early on. Before you and I—" He didn't finish.

"How is Mayor Chamberlain?"

"Talkative." Daniel twisted his fork in the lo mein

noodles on his plate, forcing himself to eat, though his earlier hunger had faded into a sort of queasy emptiness.

Rose picked up her fork again and ate the speared shrimp. The next few minutes passed in silence as they slowly made a dent in the food on their plates.

Finally, Rose put down her fork. "McBride didn't believe in Lily's visions when they first met."

Daniel took a sip of tea. "I know."

"He had his reasons—good ones."

"His daughter's kidnapping," Daniel guessed, making an intuitive leap.

Her eyes narrowed. "I'm surprised he told you about that."

"He didn't."

"Then how—"

"I'm a criminal profiler, Rose. I connected the dots." He smiled. "Did you think I had some sort of psychic gift?"

He must have used the wrong words or the wrong term, because she stiffened.

"I'm not scoffing at you," he said quickly.

Her lips tightened. "Yes, you are."

He caught her chin, forcing her to look at him. "No, I'm not. But, I guess, I am trying to make a point."

She didn't say anything, but she didn't look away, either, so he continued.

"I think you're a profiler, too."

Her eyes ticked open a little wider.

"Untrained, unorthodox—but isn't that really what you do? Don't tell me the true-love veils or the death veils do it all. Insight doesn't just pop into being, fully formed like a gift from God. What you saw in those people—call it whatever you want—came from you. Your instincts. Your insights. Your ability to read human behavior, body language, verbal cues, all of it. You had it, and then, when you got it wrong with the Granvilles, you lost faith in it. So you think they went away."

"I *think* they went away," she repeated, her eyes narrowing.

"You didn't think you could trust your instincts about relationships, anymore, after what happened with the Granvilles."

He could tell by the look in her eyes that he was right. He pushed forward, needing her to understand what was becoming so plain to him the more he thought about it. "You lost faith in your instincts, so you didn't see true-love veils anymore."

"You think I never saw true-love veils, at all," she murmured, her back straightening. "You think I was just reading body language and—and that's where I'm not following."

"Did you ever stop believing in magic?" he asked, meeting her wary gaze. "When you were a kid, I mean."

She looked down at her plate. "You think I'm delusional."

"No, I think you have a different definition of insight."

She shook her head. "I know what insight is. Insight is what tells me you're scared to death of buying into anything you can't measure or quantify or stick under a microscope." She leaned toward him. "What happened, you saw Bigfoot in the woods and all the other guys laughed at you?"

Now she was spooking him. "I saw the ghost of my

grandfather at his funeral," he said. "Or, what I called a ghost at the time. But, now I know, I imagined seeing him because my memories of him were so strong and my emotions were so high."

"So the veils are my mind's way of explaining what my intuition is trying to tell me?" She arched one dark eyebrow. "I'll give you this—it's an elegant explanation. Simple, but broad, covers any number of possible phenomena. Of course, it would work better if I were still twelve years old, but—"

The trill of a cell phone interrupted her. She fell silent, her gaze tangling with his. He reached into his pocket and pulled out his phone, checking the display. It was Steve, working late. He thumbed the phone on. "What's up, Steve?"

"I found something interesting about Jesse Phillips. I've e-mailed it to you. See what you think and call me back if you want me to keep digging."

Daniel hung up and looked at Rose. "I've got mail."

ROSE PEERED OVER Daniel's shoulder, scanning the e-mail from his assistant. "He changed his name?"

"Looks that way," Daniel murmured. "Twelve years ago he was Jesse Pennington."

"Is that significant?"

"Maybe." Daniel jotted a quick note to Steve, asking him to dig deeper into the background of Jesse Pennington and closed the e-mail program.

"Do you think the security company knows?" she asked.

"Probably wouldn't matter unless he had a record as Jesse Pennington."

"So this might be unimportant?"

Daniel shook his head. "Too soon to say." He opened his phone and dialed a number. After a pause, he said, "Captain Green, it's Daniel Hartman. You may know this already, but I've come across some information about Jesse Phillips."

As Daniel told the captain what he'd learned, Rose sat back in her chair, a strange numbness working its way through her limbs. "Thirteen years ago. That's about when the murders started, right?" she asked Daniel when he hung up the phone.

"Yes."

The numb sensation reached her fingers and toes. "It's him, isn't it?"

Daniel turned to look at her. "There's no way to say at this point—"

"I started getting the notes the day after I met Jesse Phillips at the neighborhood meeting. He put the security systems in Alice's apartment and Melissa's house. Plus, I've seen multiple death veils in his presence, twice now." She raised one trembling hand to her mouth, as if she could hold back the helpless smile curving her lips. "It has to be him."

"He's looking better for it," Daniel admitted, putting his hands on her knees. "But if he's Orion, he knows what he's doing. It'll take solid evidence to put him away—a lot more than just doing his job and changing his name, both of which are perfectly legal. Don't drop your guard yet."

She caught his hands in hers. "Can't I be happy for a few minutes? Can't I feel normal for one night?"

His thumb brushed the back of her hand. "As long

as you can feel normal without leaving this house, yeah. Have at it."

She smiled at him suddenly. "Do you dance?"

His eyebrows quirked. "No."

She laughed, jumping up and pulling him to his feet. "Well, tonight, you do."

Chapter Fourteen

Daniel didn't recognize the woman dancing around the living room. This Rose Browning glowed with life as she stepped and swayed to the driving beat of a Dierks Bentley song. Dierks hit the chorus with gusto, and Rose's hair slid out of the tidy twist at the base of her head, spilling across her shoulders.

She'd shed her suit jacket as soon as she'd reached the living room, revealing a lacy, blue, sleeveless camisole beneath. Her shoes had been the next bit of apparel to go, ending up on opposite ends of the living room with two quick kicks in rhythm with the music.

She turned to look at him, her eyes alive with frantic energy. "Come on, Daniel. Don't be a wallflower."

He shook his head, smiling at her energy. "That adrenaline rush is going to wear off in a few minutes, and I'll need all my energy to carry you upstairs to bed."

She pouted, a sexy little thrust of her bottom lip that sent shockwaves straight to his groin. She danced her way across the room to the CD player and punched the advance button a couple of times. The husky baritone of Dierks Bentley disappeared, replaced by a slow, sexy Trisha Yearwood ballad.

Rose held out her hand, her eyes warm with invitation. He couldn't have resisted if he wanted to.

He pulled her into the circle of his arms, sliding his hand down her back until it settled just above the curve of her buttocks. He pressed her close, releasing a long sigh of pleasure as she melted into him, her arms sliding around his neck. She rested her forehead against his jaw, her breath hot against his throat.

"There. That's not so bad, is it?" she murmured.

He tangled his fingers in her hair, breathing in the tangy sea scent lingering in the dark waves. It reminded him of the sight of her sleeping on top of the covers of her bed, too exhausted to bother sliding between the sheets.

Had it been only that morning? It seemed a lifetime had passed since he'd pulled a chair up next to her bed that morning to watch her sleep.

Rose's lips brushed the side of his neck, soft and moist, eliciting a groan from somewhere deep in his chest. His hand slid lower down her back to pull her hips flush with his, pressing his growing hardness against her soft heat.

A guttural sound escaped her lips in a rush of hot breath against his flesh. She lost the slow beat of the ballad, rocking her hips against his in primal rhythm that his body recognized instantly.

Curling his fingers in her hair, he tugged her head back and claimed her mouth in a hungry kiss. She tasted of sweet tea and spicy shrimp, her tongue dancing against his, demanding more. His body responded with a surge of longing that made his head spin. He needed to be inside her, swallowed by her slick heat.

"You sure about this?" He hardly recognized the words from his lips. Since when did he try to talk a woman out of sex?

She leaned her head back, her gaze searching his face. Was she trying to gauge his intentions?

Or was she looking for a true-love veil?

"What are you looking for, Rose?" The question spilled from his lips before he could stop it.

She looked down at his chest. "Assurances, I guess."

He expected to feel irritated by her admission. What he didn't expect was a rush of sympathy that drove out any thought of anger. He might not believe she could see death veils or true-love veils or whatever the hell she wanted to call them, but he knew they were real to her. Losing the true-love veils, however it had happened, had obviously been a crushing blow to her, and he couldn't feel anything but sorry for her pain.

He cradled her face between his hands, making her look at him. "I know, you don't want to hear this, but everybody else in the world has to roll the dice and hope for the best when it comes to relationships. Now you know how the rest of us feel."

"That may be the least romantic thing I've ever heard in my life," she murmured, but her lips curved with amusement.

He stroked her hair. "Would've fed you a smooth line, but you'd have just seen through it."

She leaned her head against his shoulder. "I hate feeling like a blind man groping in the dark."

He smoothed his hand over the curve of her hip. "Trust me, you feel nothing like a man."

She chuckled, the sound vibrating through his chest.

He wrapped his arm around her and stepped back into the rhythm of the ballad, swaying to the slow beat. "Don't overthink this, Rose. Doesn't have to be anything but a dance."

She swayed with him. "And if we don't stop at dancing?"

"We're just two people enjoying each other." He wasn't sure that was the right thing to say, but he was too honest to make promises he couldn't keep.

He'd spent the last eight years putting everything else in his life second to his need to find out who had killed Tina Carter, to make up for his unforgivable lapse in judgment that night and the days after. Maybe the arrest of Jesse Phillips was the end of the road, but he didn't know that for sure.

Until he did, he couldn't make promises to anyone. Not even himself.

Rose stepped out of his embrace, her expression thoughtful. After a moment, she gave a nod. "Okay. I can deal with that."

She held out her hand.

Heart pounding, he put his hand in hers. Her warm fingers closed around his, her grip firm and sure. His skin tingled where she touched him, pleasure radiating through him from that single point of contact. Their gazes tangled, questions asked and answered in that one breathless moment.

Then she led him out of the living room and up the stairs to her bedroom.

Rose had thought it would be easy. Sex was one of the most primal of needs, as old as history and powerful enough to keep the human race alive despite the millions of ways nature and human frailty had conspired to destroy it over the centuries.

But when Daniel's hand rose up her thigh to tangle in the fabric of her panties, her heart felt as if it would burst with sheer unadulterated terror.

She took a deep breath, willing herself not to panic. Birds and bees did it. Dogs and cats, and rabbits and—

And analyzing things was only making things worse.

Daniel's hand stilled, his fingers resting lightly against the soft skin of her inner thigh. "Are you hyperventilating?"

She looked down at him in horror. "Why do you ask?"

"Because you're hyperventilating."

She closed her eyes, mortified.

"Rose, are you a virgin?"

Her eyes flew open. "What?"

His gaze was gentle but inquisitive. "It's not an insult."

"I know that." She closed her eyes, reddening with humiliation. She knew how sex worked. She was a wedding planner. Sex was part of her business. Sort of. Plus, she was college educated, and more than one boyfriend had rounded second on his way to third over the years, thank you very much.

But the truth was, she'd waited for the true-love veil to tell her when she'd found The One.

She took another deep breath, letting anger push away the fear. No point in waiting anymore. The true-love veils were gone. They weren't coming back. As Daniel had said, real-world relationships didn't come with any guarantees.

She wanted him. That was the only truth that mattered. Even now, in the grip of sheer panic, her flesh hummed where he touched her. His dark gaze, thoughtful and intense, sent liquid heat flooding straight to her center. The only thing she feared more than making love with Daniel was not making love with him.

If he stopped now and walked away, she'd chase him down and make him put out the fire he'd slowly stoked inside her from the first time he'd met her gaze across a crowded bar.

She took his hand and slid it up her thigh until his fingers pressed against her center. A jolt of white-hot pleasure shot through her, eliciting a soft gasp.

Pressing a kiss against her hip, Daniel slipped his fingers inside her panties and touched her. Her breath caught.

"I'm not in any hurry here," he murmured against her belly, dropping a light kiss beside her navel.

Evidence to the contrary pressed heavy and hard against her leg, but she couldn't have found her voice to argue even if she wanted to. What his hands were doing to her body was sheer genius, leaving her no hope of having a coherent thought.

He was relentless, driving her toward madness with each touch, each kiss, each murmured word of endearment against her skin. He tugged her panties down her legs and tossed them aside, kissing his way back up her legs. Sensation melted into sensation, each more intense than the last, until something inside her splintered into a thousand shards of pleasure, leaving her shaking and breathless.

Daniel wrapped his arms around her, holding her until the shudders eased. "You okay?" he whispered.

She managed a nod, still too shaken to speak.

Daniel stroked her hair and rolled away, sitting on the side of the bed. He reached for his jacket, which he'd draped over the back of a nearby chair. "I bought these today, before I went to get dinner." He showed her a small box of condoms. "Just in case."

She couldn't help smiling. Confident devil.

"It's still not too late to stop," he murmured, although she could tell by the look of consternation on his face that he couldn't believe he was actually saying those words.

She took the box from him and pulled out a foil wrapper. This she could handle. In her line of business, she'd been to enough bachelorette parties to know what to do with a condom.

"Lose the pants." Her voice sounded raw.

Arching an eyebrow, Daniel stepped out of his trousers. His underwear quickly followed. Slowly, he turned to face her.

Her hands began to shake, her bravado leaching away.

"Small steps, sugar." Daniel took the condom from her trembling fingers and sheathed himself. He sat beside her on the bed, smoothing her hair away from her damp face.

"I know what to expect," she said.

He smiled. "No, you don't." He bent and kissed her,

the touch light and sweet enough to bring tears to her eyes.

He dropped kisses across her jawline and down the side of her neck. He dipped his tongue into the hollow of her throat and moved lower, each touch of his mouth to her flesh painting streaks of fire across her skin.

She shifted restlessly, her back arching as his erection pressed against her belly. A hot ache settled in her center and radiated outward, driving out her fear. She dropped her hands to his hips, guiding him between her thighs. When he entered her, the breath rushed from her lungs in a low, growling moan.

She wasn't sure what she'd expected. Pain, certainly, but that was mild and ephemeral, quickly eclipsed by a kaleidoscope of sensations, constantly splintering and reforming new, more vibrant colors and shapes and sounds. Pressure built inside her, a gathering firestorm. Heat licked at her belly, crackled and sizzled through her blood until the flash fire consumed her.

Daniel moved over her, into her, through her, carrying her with him as he soared toward release. She dug her fingers into his back, holding on as he lost himself inside her.

She didn't want to let him go. Couldn't let him go.

Silence descended between them, as slow and sure as the daylight dying outside her window. As their ragged respirations eased, she once again could hear the normal sounds of her life seep into her bedroom. The hum of electricity moving through the walls. The rumble of traffic from the expressway a few blocks away. The slow plink-plink of the dripping faucet in the bathroom sink across the hall.

Daniel tucked her against him, cupping one breast in his hand. He stroked her nipple with the pad of his thumb, the caress somehow more tender than sexual. "Still with me?"

"Still here," she answered, her voice raspy.

He didn't say anything else, just rested his chin on her shoulder, his breath warm on her cheek. His beard stubble pricked her skin, the sensation more pleasant than painful.

Rose curled up closer to him, drowsiness descending. She felt as if her body were an alien landscape of shifting sands trembling with aftershocks, spinning out of control into a deep, endless darkness, wondrous and frightening at the same time.

She closed her eyes and shut out the night, shut out the doubts and hopes that clamored for her attention.

Something had happened tonight. Something big and important. But she was too wrung out to think about it yet.

There was plenty of time.

DANIEL LISTENED to Rose's slow, deep respirations, his own body begging for sleep. But he had too much to think about to give in to post-sex lethargy.

He eased himself away, careful not to wake her, and gathered up his clothes, carrying them with him into the bathroom across the hall. He closed the door behind him and leaned against it, his heart thudding against his rib cage.

It was supposed to have been just sex. Two healthy, consenting adults enjoying nature's oldest full-contact sport. No promises, no expectations.

No virgins.

He flicked on the light switch and gazed at his reflection in the mirror. His jaw was dark with the day's growth of beard, his eyes sunken and a little bloodshot from lack of sleep and a heavy dose of second thoughts.

He hadn't forced her to do anything. He'd offered to stop more than once. She'd seemed pretty happy with the outcome, he thought, his lips curving with a wry half smile.

So if it wasn't her state of mind he was worried about, whose was it? His own?

You're scared because she matters.

God help him, she mattered in a way nobody had mattered to him in a long, long time. He'd spent the last hour doing everything he knew to please her, hardly even caring whether or not he got what he needed out of their intimacy. That wasn't normal. Hell, it wasn't *natural.* His neatly ordered world was spinning out of control in the wrong direction.

It scared the hell out of him.

He pushed away from the door and turned on the shower, cranking up the hot water until steam filled the small bathroom. He grabbed a cloth from the shelf over the toilet and picked up a bar of soap from the sink. The last thing he needed was to use the sea-scented bath gel sitting in the shower caddy; the tangy-sweet smell of her already covered him from head to toe.

He stepped into the tub, wincing as the fiery needles of water peppered his skin. He soaped up, scrubbing his skin as if he could somehow remove the feel of her softness against his flesh. But the mere thought of her lying beneath him, open and willing to take what he offered and give back in return made him hard all over again.

With an angry gesture, he turned off the hot water and cranked up the cold. The icy spray made him gasp, but it eased the ache between his legs enough for him to regain control. He turned off the water and stepped out into the steamy bathroom.

He toweled off and dressed, the humidity plastering his shirt to his damp skin. He escaped into the cooler air of the hallway, stopping to look into Rose's bedroom.

She lay on her side, the curve of her hips and thighs as smooth and pale as porcelain in the moonlight pouring through the window. He wanted to touch her, to let his fingers follow the curves and planes of her body once more to see if he could discover a part of her he hadn't yet explored.

He curled his treacherous hands into fists at his sides and forced himself down the hall, out of sight and temptation's reach. Moving soundlessly, he made his way through the darkened house until he reached the kitchen, where he'd left his laptop. Flicking on the light over the table, he powered up and checked his e-mail. Nothing since the message from Steve.

He shut the laptop and stared at the darkness outside the kitchen window. The clock over the table read 6:45 a.m. but it felt later. A lot had happened in the last day.

Too much.

The trill of his cell phone ripped through the silence in the kitchen, jarring his nerves. He dug in his jacket pocket and thumbed it on. "Hartman."

"Hartman, this is Sheila Green. Phillips is making noise about lawyering up, but he hasn't said the magic words yet. We think he might break with the right questions. It's time to put your voodoo to work. Can you be here in the next ten minutes?"

"Can you make it twenty?" He needed time to get Rose up and in the shower, first.

"I'm not sure we have twenty."

Daniel ran his hand over his face. He didn't like the thought of leaving Rose here alone, but if he didn't head out in the next couple of minutes, he might not get a chance to question Phillips. "Okay, I'll be there in ten."

He hurried upstairs to the bedroom. Rose was still asleep, her face soft and peaceful. He hated to wake her, but he needed to make sure she locked up behind him. "Rose?"

She blinked awake, squinting as he turned on the bedside lamp. "What's wrong?"

"I have to get to police headquarters in ten minutes. I need to try to break Phillips before he asks for his lawyer."

She rubbed her eyes. "He hasn't called his lawyer?"

"Some perps like to play head games with the cops awhile before bringing in a mouthpiece. I'd rather take you, but I don't have time for you to shower and dress." He grabbed the robe hanging behind her door and handed it to her. "I need you to lock up behind me."

She shrugged on the robe. "Any idea when you'll be back?"

Part of him wanted to play it safe and go back to the motel, instead. He pushed the fear aside. Whatever he chose to do about Rose, she still needed his protection. "I'll call."

She followed him to the back door, her expression hard to read. He thought he saw confusion and a hint of disappointment, but he didn't have time to ferret out the rest of the chaos of emotions flickering in her mossy-brown eyes. "Lock up behind me," he repeated, opening the door.

She gazed up at him. "Drive carefully."

He kissed her forehead, knowing it was all he could allow himself if he wanted to get to the police station in the next few minutes. And even that simple gesture of affection was enough to reawaken a slow-simmering ache of longing that tormented him with each step he took away from her.

Damn, he was in serious trouble.

ROSE CLOSED HER EYES and raised her face to the shower spray, letting the water wash away the hot tears sliding down her cheeks. She didn't even have the luxury of anger; after all, Daniel had been pretty clear about things, hadn't he? *We're just two people enjoying each other.*

And she'd definitely enjoyed it. The things his hands and mouth had done to her body would stay with her for a long time. Hot water and bath gel did nothing to erase the smell of him, the musky heat of his skin on hers, over her, inside her, driving her insane with need. No complaints there.

But did he really have to run out chasing the case before she'd even stopped trembling from her climax? That was veering dangerously into "slam, bam, thank you, ma'am" territory.

It was her own damned fault. Pretending she was sophisticated enough to handle casual sex with a man obsessed with a dead woman and her killer.

There were a lot of women who were fine with that, and more power to them. She just wasn't one of them. She wanted sex to be more than a couple of bodies doing what nature intended. She wanted to mean more to Daniel than that.

Obviously, she didn't.

She finished rinsing shampoo from her hair and shut off the water. The tears were back, leaving hot tracks down her cheeks as she stepped onto the bath mat. She wrapped a towel around herself and stood in front of the sink. In the foggy mirror, her reflection was a blob of light on dark, unrecognizable. She grabbed a hand towel and wiped the condensation from the mirror.

A second later, the towel slipped from her nerveless fingers and puddled in the sink.

The death veil was back.

Chapter Fifteen

"He's been released?" Daniel stared at Captain Green.

"Five minutes before you got here."

"Why didn't you call me?"

"We did. Kept getting your voice mail." Sheila Green gave him a pointed look.

Daniel checked his cell phone, horrified to find it off. What if Rose had been trying to call him? He thumbed through the messages and found two from Captain Green but none from Rose. He let himself relax. "Why'd you let him go?"

"He had a solid alibi for last night's murder, and a plausible one for the Donovan murder. Those were the only two we could remotely connect him to, so we had to cut him loose."

"That doesn't mean he didn't kill the other two."

"It doesn't mean he did, either."

Daniel sighed, frustrated. He'd blown off Rose to come here, not even an hour after making love with her. She must be furious. Or hurt. Or both. "What about the name change?"

"He had a nervous breakdown when he was twenty,

ended up in an institution for a few months. Said he changed his name as soon as he got out to turn a new page in his life." Green shrugged. "He gave us permission to check with the hospital where he was institutionalized. They faxed over the admission date, confirming it." She handed him a sheet of paper.

The date at the top caught his eye. "April 14th."

"Does that mean something?"

Tina had been killed the night of April 13th. "Maybe. Did Phillips say what caused his breakdown?"

"School pressures—he was having trouble in college."

"Did he mention a girlfriend—a bad breakup or anything like that?"

"No. He was pretty vague about it."

"What college? Maybe he spoke to a counselor there."

"U.A.B."

Same as Tina, Daniel thought. Might be significant. Had Tina ever told him about someone named Jesse Pennington? He couldn't remember. While he was away at college, they'd mostly corresponded by mail. She hadn't wanted to run up a big phone bill with her family on a limited income.

Had she mentioned Jesse's name in any of her notes to him?

"I need to check on something." He waved the sheet of paper at Captain Green. "Can I get a copy of this for my file?"

"Sure." She frowned. "Does it mean something to you?"

"I don't know," he admitted, "but I'm about to find out."

Rose stared at the shimmer over her reflection, trying to convince herself she was imagining it. But the streaks of crimson bleeding through the silver remained no matter how hard she blinked her eyes.

Outside, the weather had worsened, wind rattling her rain-streaked windowpanes. A flash of lightning strobed the sky, lighting up her bedroom as she scrambled for the phone on her bedside table. She picked up the receiver.

There was no dial tone.

She turned on the bedside lamp. Warm yellow light spread across the darkened room. She slumped on the side of her bed. At least, she wasn't stuck without a phone in a darkened house.

She dressed quickly in jeans and a cashmere pullover. The soft sweater was warm and soft against her damp skin, easing some of the shivers rattling through her.

But not all of them.

She forced herself to check the dresser mirror. The death veil remained. What did it mean? Was Jesse Phillips not the killer, after all?

Daniel would know, she realized. Where was her cell phone? Mentally she retraced her steps. She'd had it when she came in with Lily—and put it on the kitchen counter.

The moan of the wind followed her to the staircase, howling around the eaves. Halfway down, the lights went off, the ambient hum of electricity dying away. Rose detoured to the front door, peering through the glass side pane. The streetlamps were dark. The whole block was without power.

Perversely, seeing evidence of the power outage

made her feel marginally better as she felt her way along the hall to the kitchen. At least, she could stop worrying that someone outside had cut her power. Relaxing, she stepped through the doorway.

And froze.

The back door stood wide-open, rain slanting inside.

Rose went utterly still, listening. Wind moaned through the trees outside, rain clattering against the concrete patio. She heard nothing else, save her own harsh breathing and the rapid-fire pulse in her ears.

She edged toward the counter where she'd left her cell phone. Minimal light flowed in through the open door, barely enough to make out the pale granite countertop. She felt her way along the counter, fingers flexing in search of the phone.

It wasn't there.

No time to look for it. She had to get out now. Where were her car keys?

She'd left her purse on one of the kitchen chairs, she remembered. She padded silently to the other side of the room and groped for the chair. Her hand tangled in her purse strap.

Then she heard the front door open.

Her fingers went numb, the purse sliding from her grasp. Panic blackened the edges of her vision.

Someone was in the house.

DANIEL TURNED OFF Clairmont Avenue and headed up the hill past the Lakeview Golf Course, his headlights bouncing off the driving rain. As he turned left onto his mother's street, he tried Rose's cell phone again. Still no answer. Her home phone wasn't working, either. He told himself it was the storm.

He almost believed it.

The two-story brick house had been his childhood home. He parked in front and sat for a moment, staring up at the familiar facade. He hadn't been back since his dad's funeral, he realized. What kind of son would let so much time pass between visits with his mother?

Pushing himself out of the car, he raced through the rain up the front walk and rang the bell.

Footsteps approached and the porch light came on. A moment later the front door opened. His mother stood in the entrance, older and frailer than he remembered.

"Hi, Mom."

Dinah Hartman stepped back to let him in. "What's wrong?"

He stared at her a moment, shamed by the question. That she'd think something had to be wrong for him to visit—

Except, that was exactly the case, wasn't it?

He started to give her a hug, then realized his suit jacket was dripping wet. He settled for kissing her cheek. The soft powder scent of her brought back an overwhelming rush of memories. He pushed them away before they paralyzed him. "Nothing's wrong. Least, I hope not."

He shrugged out of his jacket, tossing it toward the coatrack, which had stood in the foyer as long as he could remember. It fell to the floor.

"I moved the coatrack," Dinah Hartman murmured, picking up the jacket. She folded it and draped it over the new hall table. "Been in town long?"

"A few weeks," he admitted, hating the look of resignation in her eyes. "Should've called earlier."

"Yes, you should've." She started toward the living room.

He caught her arm. "Actually, I need to know where you stored all my old stuff."

ROSE CROUCHED AND GRABBED for the purse she'd dropped, moaning as some of the contents spilled to the floor. Ignoring the mess, she felt for the keys. They rattled under her fingers, sending terror jolting through her. Had he heard?

She grabbed the keys and scrambled out the back door, sprinting through the sheeting rain. Something loomed out of the darkness, right into her path. She hit a solid wall of denim and leather. A pair of hands curled around her arms, pinning her in place. She opened her mouth to scream.

"Shh, it's me." Frank Carter's voice, low and tense, froze the breath in her lungs. "Is he in there?"

Rose blinked away the rain stinging her eyes. "I don't know. I locked the back door, but it was open, and I heard the front door open and shut—"

"We let Phillips go. I was following him but he shook my tail. I came here on a hunch." Frank motioned toward the alley and handed Rose a set of keys. He pulled a gun from a holster hidden inside his leather jacket. "Get in my car and lock it. I'll check your house."

Rose hesitated, not sure she was ready to be alone, even in a locked car. But Frank was already moving toward the house.

Rose scurried up the steps and unlocked the sedan

parked behind her Chevy. She slid into the passenger seat, locked all the doors and slumped low in the seat, shivering.

Movement in her backyard caught her gaze. Frank was coming up the steps toward the car. His gun was in its holster; he obviously hadn't found anyone inside. She let him in, handing over the keys.

"I found signs of breaking and entering, but he's gone. I'll send a squad car out when we get to H.Q."

"Can't you call it in on the radio?"

"I'm off duty. I don't have a radio in my personal car."

"Can I use your cell phone? I need to call Daniel."

"Sure." He handed over his phone and started the car.

She punched the on button but nothing happened. "Am I doing something wrong?"

Frank took the phone from her and gave it a try. "Piece of crap battery." He leaned toward the glove box but pulled back, muttering a curse. "My charger's in my department car."

"I'll catch up with him at the police station."

"Do you mind if we stop by my house, first, to get another battery? It's a quick detour. I'd rather avoid another lecture from my captain about keeping equipment up to date."

"I don't mind," she assured him.

She just wanted to get as far away from her house as possible.

DANIEL STARED at the boxes lining the basement shelves. "All that's mine?"

"Yours, mine, your father's, your brother's…" Dinah

shrugged. "If I'd only known to organize it, in case you dropped by."

He slanted a look at his mother, noting her sly smile. Suddenly she didn't seem nearly as old or fragile as he'd thought when she first opened the door. "Touché."

"If you tell me what we're looking for, I'll help."

"I'm looking for some old letters from Tina Carter." Daniel pulled the closest box from the shelf and put it on the table. "Want to see if she mentioned someone in her letters."

The humor left his mother's face. She pulled down a second box. "Does this have to do with the Southside killer?"

Daniel looked up, surprised.

"You think I couldn't guess why you're here? You're a profiler. There's a murderer loose."

"We have a suspect in the case. Turns out he went to high school with Tina, and had a breakdown the day after her murder." Daniel riffled through the box in front of him quickly, finding nothing. He reached for another box.

"This looks like something from Tina." Dinah held up a piece of paper. "There are several in here."

Daniel took the note from her. She was right; it was from Tina. He took the box from her and handed a stack of the letters to his mother, taking another stack for himself. "Look for the name Jesse Pennington anywhere in the notes."

She looked reluctant. "Sure you want me to read these?"

He nodded, already scanning another letter.

A few moments later he came across an envelope that was still sealed. The date stamp was April 8.

Five days before Tina's death.

The faded memory came back to him. He'd received a letter from Tina the afternoon he'd been packing up for a weekend trip home. Since he'd see her in a few hours, he'd tucked the note into his backpack and forgot about it until after her death.

He'd never been able to talk himself into opening it.

Slowly, he slid his finger under the flap and opened the envelope. Taking a deep breath, he pulled out the letter tucked inside and unfolded it.

The first few paragraphs were standard greetings and professions of affection, written in Tina's neat, girlish script. But a couple of paragraphs down, he saw the name he was looking for.

Jesse Pennington from my psych class won't stop asking me out. I told him I have a fiancé, but he said you've probably got a half-dozen girls at Vandy. You don't, do you?

"Did you find something?" his mother asked. Nodding, he read the rest of it silently.

He's so intense. I swear, I think he thinks he's the one I'm supposed to marry or something. Maybe I could introduce you to him this weekend so he'll know I'm not just making you up.

Daniel stared at the letter, numbness spreading over him in tingly waves.

It was right here. The answer had been right here in Tina's letter the whole time. If he hadn't been such a coward, if he'd made himself open the letter and face the guilt and shame, he could have given the police an invaluable clue to the murderer's identity.

Had Jesse been stalking Tina that night and seen their fight? She'd run off—had he followed? Maybe he'd tried to make his move, been rebuffed and struck out in hurt and rage. Wouldn't be the first time a broken heart led to a murder.

Daniel picked up his phone and dialed Captain Green's number. When she answered, he told her what he'd found. "You need to bring Phillips back in for more questioning. Ask him about Tina Carter's murder."

"Will do," Green said.

Daniel hung up and started to fold the letter when the notepaper style suddenly caught his eye. The paper was a bit faded, but the silver butterflies lining the edge of the paper were unmistakable.

It looked like the same paper the killer had used to send his notes to Rose, he realized.

He pulled out his phone and dialed Captain Green. "Me again. Lab have anything yet on the notepaper?"

"Yeah, something just came in." There was a pause filled with rustling noises. "Yeah, they've ID'd the notepaper. Butterfly Symphony, from the Signature Expressions series available by special order about fourteen years ago exclusively from Magic City Paper here in town. The brand was available for two years and then discontinued."

Special order, Daniel thought, his chest tightening. "What about the cut part of the note?"

"The lab tech notes the original notepaper had a rectangular section at the bottom where the owner's name would have been printed. Our guy must've cut it off because it could identify him in some way."

Daniel looked down at the notepaper in his hand. There at the bottom was a pale silver rectangle with Tina's name embossed across it. His heart skipped a beat. "Is Frank Carter there?"

"No," Captain Green answered. "He left right after we let Phillips go. I'm about to call him to pick up Phillips—you want him to give you a call?"

Daniel's chest tightened. "Yeah. Do that." He hung up, his stomach coiling into a knot.

"You think this Jesse person is the Southside killer?"

Daniel's looked into his mother's troubled eyes. "I think he killed Tina. But I don't know if he killed the others."

"I INHERITED this house from my mother," Frank told Rose as he led her into the small foyer of the brick bungalow. The house was spotless, the air fragrant with a lemony-clean smell. "She died this past spring."

Frank led her down a narrow hallway to a room near the back. All the hallway doors were open but one that bore a fading sign tacked into the white painted wood: No Brothers Allowed. Frank gave the door a wide berth as he passed.

The shrine, Rose thought.

They reached a back room, which Frank used as an office. Unlike the rest of the house, this room looked lived in. Papers and bills lay in stacks on the other end of the desk. A touch-tone phone sat at one end—not cordless, Rose noted, but a model from a decade or more ago. The house had frozen in time thirteen years ago. "May I use your phone?" she asked.

"Sure." Frank started searching one of the drawers.

Rose picked up the phone. There was no dial tone. She toggled the switch hook without luck. "It's not working."

Frank looked up. "What?" He took the phone she handed him, rattling the switch hook himself. He frowned. "Old house. When I find a battery, you can use my cell phone."

Rose sighed and sat in the desk chair. Lightning flashed outside, followed by a rattling boom of thunder that made her jump. Her hand knocked a cardboard box off the desk. It opened when it hit, spilling its contents. Silver-embossed notepaper scattered around her feet.

Her heart stuttered.

"Damn," Frank murmured behind her. "I wasn't ready for you to see that."

Chapter Sixteen

Rose turned to look at Frank, feigning ignorance, even as her heart started galloping. "Sorry, did you say something?"

Frank dropped his gaze to the notepaper on the floor. It wasn't much of a distraction, but Rose didn't dare wait for a better one. She darted for the door.

Frank caught up with her in the doorway and jerked her to him. Rose brought her knee up, missing his groin but hitting his thigh. Grunting, he wrapped his fingers in her hair.

"Gotta do better than that," he growled. His breath stank of black coffee and peppermint. "You all try to run."

She slumped against him. He shifted to keep from overbalancing, giving her the opening she needed. She brought her knee up again, this time hitting him square between the legs. He grunted, his grip loosening.

She followed with a hard jab of the heel of her hand into his nose. He lost his hold on her, and she ran. He recovered quickly, gaining behind her.

She'd never make the front door, she realized.

But as she reached the door to Tina's room, she heard Daniel's voice as clearly as if he were beside her. *Frank hated that room. Couldn't bring himself to go in there.*

She skidded to a stop, grabbed the doorknob and lifted a prayer. Then she slipped inside, slamming the door behind her.

"YOU WANT WHAT?" Captain Green sounded incredulous.

"An A.P.B. on Frank Carter." Daniel parked at the back of Rose's house, relieved to see her car in the usual place.

"Just because he's not answering his phone?"

"The notepaper the killer is using to send notes to Rose is the same notepaper his sister used to use." Outlining what he'd discovered at his mother's house, he got out of his car. "I don't think it can be a coincidence."

"My God." Captain Green's voice came out strangled.

The block was dark; the power was out. He grabbed a flashlight from his trunk. "We can sort it out once we find Frank. Get the A.P.B. issued. I'll call you back." He hurried down the steps to the house and tried the back door. It was locked. He knocked hard, hoping Rose was still awake. When she didn't answer, he tried her cellphone number again. A moment later, he heard a faint ringing sound behind him.

He rounded the side of the house, following the sound. He caught sight of a pale blue glow a few feet ahead. His heart in his throat, he took another step forward and looked down.

Rose's cell phone lay in the wet grass, still ringing.

TINA'S DOOR had a push-button privacy lock, but Rose knew it wouldn't stop Frank for long. She pressed it anyway and dashed to the only window in the room. Daniel had said Tina used to climb through the window to meet him on the wraparound porch. She tried the window. It didn't budge. On closer inspection, she discovered it had been nailed shut from the outside.

Slumping against the sill, she gazed toward the door. She could hear Frank's shallow, harsh breathing just outside. But he still hadn't tried the door.

She surveyed the room. Photos of Tina and friends lined the oval vanity mirror across from the bed. A shelf above the dresser held several awards—cheerleading trophies, certificates of merit, even a small jewel-encrusted tiara sitting atop a folded white sash.

Mama's little princess, Rose thought, not unkindly.

"Come out of there!" Frank's sudden angry bark ripped at her nerves.

She remained silent, wondering how long Frank's fear of his sister's ghost would keep him at bay. Sooner or later, he'd screw up his courage and burst through the door.

Better be ready.

She looked around for something to use as a weapon. A baton leaned against the closet door, a pitiful excuse for a weapon. A softball bat would have been a big help.

"Why couldn't you have been a tomboy?" she muttered.

Her gaze settled on an old-fashioned princess phone on the bedside table. It looked heavy enough to hurt.

Grabbing the phone, she missed, knocking the receiver from the hook.

And heard a dial tone.

BREAKING THROUGH Rose's back door was depressingly easy. He turned on the flashlight and surveyed the kitchen. Objects lay scattered on the floor—a lipstick, papers and a billfold. Hands shaking, he opened the billfold with his fingertip. Rose's driver's license photo stared back at him from inside.

He pushed to his feet, his chest aching with dread. "Rose, are you in here?" He started searching the house, terrified of what he might find just around the corner. Halfway up the steps to the second floor, his cell phone rang. A local number, no name attached. It looked familiar, so he answered. "Hartman."

"Daniel, it's me." Rose's voice whispered in his ear.

He grabbed the stair railing to keep from falling backward. "Are you okay? I can barely hear you."

"I'm in Tina's room," she said.

His legs gave out on him and he sat in the middle of the stairs. "Tina's room?"

"Frank's outside. I think he's afraid to come in here." Her voice broke. "Please come get me."

Her plea tumbling through his mind, he scrambled to his feet and down the stairs, two at a time. "I'm coming. Just hold on!" He flew through the darkened house to the back door and up the sloping yard to his car. He cranked the engine. "I'm coming, Rose—can you hear me?"

"Frank's the Southside killer," she whispered.

"I know." He peeled out of the alley onto the street.

"Tell me what to do." Her voice was tight with fear. "He said I looked like her. Can I do something with that?"

Daniel couldn't think. He should be able to think, damn it! It was his job. He was good at it. But now, when it mattered more than anything in the world, he couldn't think.

"You said he's afraid of her ghost." On Rose's end, Daniel heard the sound of a door opening.

His heart froze. "Rose?"

"I opened the closet. There are tons of clothes here. I think I can fit into something."

Daniel took a curve too quickly, the back end of his car fishtailing. He dropped the phone to the seat beside him and steered out of the skid. He grabbed the phone again. "Rose?"

"I'll call you back." With a click, the connection ended.

He started to hit the redial button but stopped. The phone ringing might break through Frank's hesitation. He couldn't risk it. He punched in Captain Green's number instead. Tersely outlining the situation, he asked her to send units to Frank's address. "Approach with care. He has a hostage."

Hanging up, he weaved through the traffic on Highland Avenue, willing Rose to call him back.

ROSE SMOOTHED the plaid skirt over her hips, checking her reflection in the mirror on the closet door. The tartan skirt and navy cable-knit sweater would give Frank the fright of his life if he decided to break through that door.

"You have to come out sooner or later," Frank warned. "Mama nailed the window shut." He laughed, low and harsh. "The window had let her little princess out that night. Bad window."

Ignoring his taunts, Rose picked up the phone and dialed Daniel's number.

He answered immediately. "Rose?"

He sounded so frantic, she thought, tears stinging her eyes. "He's getting angry. He wants me to go out there."

"Good. He's still afraid to come in there."

"Should I be talking to him?"

Daniel was silent.

"Daniel?"

His voice dropped to a growl. "I can't lose you, Rose."

She sank onto the bed, her heart contracting. Tears welled in her eyes, painting the room in hazy watercolors. "Daniel," she whispered, her throat tight with emotion.

Her cleared his throat. "Don't talk to him unless he comes in before I get there. Then, talk about the murders. He'll want to tell someone what he's done. It'll buy you time."

A bang on the door made her jump. "I think he's tired of waiting," she whispered. "I better hang up—"

"No, don't hang up! Put the phone down but leave the receiver off the cradle so I can hear what's going on."

She put the receiver on the table as another thud hit the door, accompanied by the sound of splintering wood. She crouched behind the bed, peering over the edge.

The lock gave and Frank lurched into the room, a large knife in his hand. He stumbled to a stop and stared at her, taking in the sight of Rose in his sister's clothes. His face blanching, he backpedaled into the door. "Tina," he whispered.

Rose lifted her chin. "Frankie, what've you done?"

As DANIEL SLAMMED to a stop in front of Frank's house, he heard the sound of wood splintering through the phone. He parked at a haphazard angle, shut off the engine and scrambled out. Rain drowned out Rose's end of the call, propelling him up the porch to the front door. It was unlocked.

It would be smarter to wait for police backup, but he didn't have time. Pulling his SIG-Sauer from his hip holster, he slipped inside, leaving the door open behind him.

Rose's voice drifted toward him. "I understand Alice and the others. They looked like me. But the blonde—"

"It's Rose's fault." Bitterness edged Frank's voice. "I thought she knew what I was supposed to do." His voice dropped an octave. "But she lied. She didn't have a plan."

Daniel crept toward Tina's room, his gut tightening. It had been a long time since he'd been in that room. Peeking around the door frame, he took in the lay of things. Frank stood just in front of him, wielding a hunting knife, his back to the door. Tina stood behind the bed, staring her brother down.

He blinked the rainwater out of his eyes. No. Not

Tina. It couldn't be Tina. It was Rose in a plaid skirt and navy sweater, a delicate jeweled tiara in her dark, wet hair.

Standing behind the shimmery figure of Tina Carter.

Rose's gaze shifted to meet his. Her eyelids flickered but she looked away quickly, showing no other sign of recognition. If she saw the ghost of Tina, she didn't show it.

Daniel flattened against the wall just outside the door, tightening his grip on the SIG-Sauer. His heart rat-a-tatted against his chest, his breath a distant memory.

A faint wail of sirens in the distance spurred him out of his paralysis. Once Frank heard the police approaching, he would be that much more dangerous.

As he started to move, Rose's next words froze him in place. "Why did you kill me?"

"I didn't." Frank's voice came out soft as a kitten's mewl. "Not the first time. Just dozens of times since then."

Daniel pressed his back to the wall. So he was right. All these years, when he'd been chasing Orion from state to state, he'd never been after Tina's killer at all.

But he could live with that.

Daniel swung around the doorway, his SIG leveled at Frank's back. "Drop the knife, Frank."

Frank pivoted, staring at Daniel with hollow eyes. He put the knife to his own throat. "She's here." His voice shook.

"I know." Daniel moved closer. "Put down the knife."

"Put it down, Frankie." Tina's voice floated through the room, tremulous and soft.

Daniel sensed movement to his right, but he kept his

gaze on Frank. Outside, sirens grew louder, then wailed to a stop. He heard the front door open.

"In here," he called, holding Frank's gaze.

"You heard her, didn't you?" Frank whispered.

Daniel nodded. "Tina wants you to put the knife down."

Slowly, the hand holding the knife trembled to Frank's side, fingers loosening. The knife thudded to the carpet as police officers poured through the doorway behind Daniel.

As they wrestled Frank to the floor, Daniel holstered his gun and stepped aside, finally allowing himself to look at Rose. She stared back at him, her eyes glittering with relief.

The apparition of Tina was gone.

He held out his hand and Rose rushed to him, throwing her arms around his waist. She buried her face in his shirt, her fingers digging into his back.

"It's over," he soothed, stroking her damp hair. He breathed in her scent, lush and female and alive. His earlier doubts and fears had fled, driven out by one inescapable truth.

He was in love with Rose Browning.

"IT'S A SLAUGHTERHOUSE down there. We should have scads of forensic evidence," Agent Brody told Daniel as he came back into the living room from a trip to the basement. He kept his voice low, but Rose heard him from her seat on the nearby sofa. She looked up at Daniel and saw him watching her, his gaze intense.

"What about Jesse Phillips? Has he said anything about Tina Carter's murder?"

"He spilled his guts. I think he was relieved to get it

out in the open. Real twelve-stepper about the whole thing—making amends and all that."

"Did he say why he did it?" Daniel asked.

"The old 'if I can't have her, nobody can' routine." Brody grimaced. "Doesn't explain why Carter killed the others, though."

"To kill Tina all over again," Rose interjected, remembering Frank's words to Daniel during the confrontation in Tina's bedroom.

Daniel looked at her, his eyes narrowed. He gave a slow nod. "I'd say that's the underlying motive, yeah."

"Well, whatever his reasons, we've got the evidence to put him away." Brody's words were laced with grim satisfaction.

So it was really over, Rose thought. All of it.

Daniel nodded toward Rose. "Can I take her home?"

"Yeah. We've got your statements. I'll be in touch."

Daniel crossed to Rose and held out his hand. "Want to change back into your clothes?"

"These are warm and dry. Unless you want me to change?"

He shook his head. "Warm and dry sounds good."

Outside, the rain had stopped, fog setting in. Daniel tucked her into the passenger seat of the Jeep, then went around to the driver's side.

"Did you really hear something?" Rose asked as he slid behind the steering wheel.

He looked at her, brow furrowed.

"You said you heard Tina tell Frank to put down the knife."

Daniel didn't say anything for a long moment. But as she started to look away, he said, "I saw her."

She whipped her gaze back to his. "Saw Tina?"

He nodded. "Standing in front of you. Didn't you?"

She shook her head, chill bumps rolling down her spine.

"I can tell myself I imagined it. I was under stress. It was her room, where I'd seen her a million times." Daniel dropped his gaze. "But it was more than that. I don't know how to explain it, but I saw her."

She touched his hand. His fingers trembled under hers.

"Did she say anything to you?" she asked.

"She just told Frank to put down the knife." Daniel smiled faintly, his gaze fixed on the fog-shrouded night visible through the windshield. "It's okay, though. I think she told me what I needed to hear."

"What's that?" She ran her thumb over the back of his hand.

Daniel exhaled slowly. "It's over. She can rest now."

"And so can you."

His gaze lifted to meet hers, and even in the dim light of the streetlamps, there was no missing the emotion shining in his eyes. "I love you. You know that, don't you?"

She blinked back tears, her heart squeezing. He reached across the console and pulled her toward him. The gearshift pressed against her hip—at least, she *thought* it was the gearshift. The thought made her chuckle as he bent to kiss her.

He pulled back. "What is it?"

She started to share the joke when something shimmery began to form over his face. Her laughter faltered, eclipsed by fear.

Not a death veil. Not now.

"Rose?" Daniel's brow furrowed beneath the shimmer.

Rose held her breath as the nascent veil coalesced into a face. She recognized the wide eyes and full lips.

They were her own.

Tears spilling down her cheeks, she cradled his face between her trembling hands. A shaky sob escaped her lips.

He covered her hands with his. "Do you see something?"

She nodded, her lips beginning to curve.

Understanding dawned. "It's not a death veil, is it?"

She shook her head, laughter spilling from her lips.

He silenced her chuckle with his mouth. She clung to him, gathering strength from his kiss. Joy infused her whole body, until she felt more alive than she'd ever felt before.

Daniel pulled back, pressing his forehead to hers. "Let me clarify—it's *your* face over mine, right?"

She chuckled, stroking his stubbled jaw. "Yes."

"So we're supposed to be together forever, right? That's how it works, isn't it?"

She thought of Dillon and Carrie Granville, a sliver of pain shooting through her chest. "It's not a guarantee."

He stroked her hair. "I don't need one."

She met his gaze. "I love you, Daniel. I didn't know how much until I heard your voice in my ear when I needed you most."

"I always want to be the voice in your ear," he murmured.

"I always want to be the woman in your bed," she replied.

He smiled. "That can definitely be arranged."

A knock on the window behind her made Rose jump. She turned to find Agent Brody staring through her window. "You two gonna neck all night or can you get your damned Jeep out of the way?" he said through the glass. "You're blocking the road."

Laughing, Daniel started the car. "Let's find a bed."

Rose sank back against the seat as he pulled away from the curb, smiling at the darkness. She didn't know if the true-love veils were back for good or if it was a one-time thing. Not that it mattered. She didn't need a true-love veil to tell her Daniel was her soul mate.

That's what her heart was for.

* * * * *

THE ROYAL HOUSE OF NIROLI
Always passionate, always proud.

The richest royal family in the world—united by blood and passion, torn apart by deceit and desire.

Nestled in the azure blue of the Mediterranean Sea, the majestic island of Niroli has prospered for centuries. The Fierezza men have worn the crown with passion and pride since ancient times. But now, as the king's health declines and his two sons have been tragically killed, the crown is in jeopardy.

The clock is ticking—a new heir must be found before the king is forced to abdicate. By royal decree the internationally scattered members of the Fierezza family are summoned to claim their destiny. But any person who takes the throne must do so according to The Rules of the Royal House of Niroli. Soon, secrets and rivalries emerge as the descendents of this ancient royal line vie for position and power. Only a true Fierezza can become ruler—a person dedicated to their country, their people...and their eternal love!

Each month starting in July 2007,
Harlequin Presents is delighted to bring you
an exciting installment from
THE ROYAL HOUSE OF NIROLI,
in which you can follow the epic search
for the true Nirolian king.
Eight heirs, eight romances, eight fantastic stories!

Here's your chance to enjoy a sneak preview of the first book delivered to you by royal decree....

FIVE minutes later she was standing immobile in front of the study's window, her original purpose of coming in forgotten, as she stared in shocked horror at the envelope she was holding. Waves of heat, followed by icy chills, surged through her body. She could hardly see the address now through her blurred vision, but the crest on its left-hand front corner stood out, its *royal* crest, followed by the address: *HRH Prince Marco of Niroli....*

She didn't hear Marco's key in the apartment door, she didn't even hear him calling out her name. Her shock was so great that nothing could penetrate it. It encased her in a kind of bubble that only concentrated the torment of what she was suffering and branded it on her brain so that it could never be forgotten. It was only finally pierced by the sudden opening of the study door as Marco walked in.

"Welcome home, *Your Highness.* I suppose I ought to curtsy." She waited, praying that he would laugh and tell her that she had got it all wrong, that the envelope she was holding, addressing him as Prince Marco of

Niroli, was some silly mistake. But like a tiny candle flame shivering vulnerably in the dark, her hope trembled fearfully. And then the look in Marco's eyes extinguished it as cruelly as a hand placed callously over a dying person's face to stem their last breath.

"Give that to me," he demanded, taking the envelope from her.

"It's too late, Marco," Emily told him brokenly. "I know the truth now…" She dug her teeth in her lower lip to try to force back her own pain.

"You had no right to go through my desk," Marco shot back at her furiously, full of loathing at being caught off guard and forced into a position in which he was in the wrong, making him determined to find something he could accuse Emily of. "I trusted you…."

Emily could hardly believe what she was hearing. "No, you didn't trust me, Marco, and you didn't trust me because you knew that I couldn't trust you. And you knew that because you're a liar and liars don't trust people because they know that they themselves cannot be trusted." She not only felt sick, she also felt as though she could hardly breathe. "You are Prince Marco of Niroli… How could you not tell me who you are and still live with me as intimately as we have lived together?" she demanded brokenly.

"Stop being so ridiculously dramatic," Marco demanded fiercely. "You are making too much of the situation."

"*Too much?*" Emily almost screamed the words at him. "When were you going to tell me, Marco? Perhaps you just planned to walk away without telling me anything? After all, what do my feelings matter to you?"

"Of course they matter." Marco stopped her sharply. "And it was in part to protect them, and you, that I'd decided not to inform you when my grandfather first announced that he intended to step down from the throne and hand it on to me."

"To protect me?" Emily nearly choked on her fury. "Hand on the throne? No wonder you told me when you first took me to bed that all you wanted was sex. You *knew* that was the only kind of relationship there could ever be between us! You *knew* that one day you would be Niroli's king. No doubt you are expected to marry a princess. Is she picked out for you already, your *royal* bride?"

* * * * *

Look for
THE FUTURE KING'S PREGNANT MISTRESS
by Penny Jordan in July 2007,
from Harlequin Presents,
available wherever books are sold.

HARLEQUIN®

Super Romance®

*Looking for a romantic, emotional
and unforgettable escape?*

*You'll find it this month and every month
with a Harlequin Superromance!*

Rory Gorenzi has a sense of humor and a sense of
honor. She also happens to be good with children.

Seamus Lee, widower and father of four, needs
someone with exactly those traits.

They meet at the Colorado mountain school owned
by Rory's father, where she teaches skiing and
avalanche safety. But Seamus—and his children—
learn more from her than that....

Look for

GOOD WITH CHILDREN

by Margot Early,

*available August 2007, and these other
fantastic titles from Harlequin Superromance.*

LOVE, BY GEORGE *Debra Salonen* #1434
THE MAN FROM HER PAST *Anna Adams* #1435
NANNY MAKES THREE *Joan Kilby* #1437
MAYBE, BABY *Terry McLaughlin* #1438
THE FAMILY SOLUTION *Bobby Hutchinson* #1439

REASONS FOR REVENGE

A brand-new provocative miniseries by *USA TODAY* bestselling author **Maureen Child** begins with

SCORNED BY THE BOSS

Jefferson Lyon is a man used to having his own way. He runs his shipping empire from California, and his admin Caitlyn Monroe runs the rest of his world. When Caitlin decides she's had enough and needs new scenery, Jefferson devises a plan to get her back. Jefferson *never* loses, but little does he know that he's in a competition....

Don't miss any of the other titles from the REASONS FOR REVENGE trilogy by *USA TODAY* bestselling author **Maureen Child.**

SCORNED BY THE BOSS #1816
Available August 2007

SEDUCED BY THE RICH MAN #1820
Available September 2007

CAPTURED BY THE BILLIONAIRE #1826
Available October 2007

Only from Silhouette Desire!

REQUEST YOUR FREE BOOKS!

2 FREE NOVELS PLUS 2 FREE GIFTS!

HARLEQUIN®

INTRIGUE®

Breathtaking Romantic Suspense

HI07

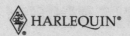

INTRIGUE

COMING NEXT MONTH

#999 NAVAJO ECHOES by Cassie Miles
Bodyguards Unlimited, Denver, CO (Book 5 of 6)
Posing as newlyweds, agents John Pinto and Lily Clark escape to the Caribbean to put Prescott Personal Securities' biggest case to rest.

#1000 A BABY BEFORE DAWN by Linda Castillo
Lights Out (Book 2 of 4)
In the throes of a blackout, Chase Vickers will risk everything to rescue his lost love, a very pregnant Lily Garrett, from some very dangerous men seeking revenge.

#1001 24 KARAT AMMUNITION by Joanna Wayne
Four Brothers of Colts Run Cross
Eldest brother L.R. knows that all the oil money in the world won't make him happy if he can't rescue his first love and find out what made her run away from Texas so long ago.

#1002 THE NEW DEPUTY IN TOWN by B.J. Daniels
Whitehorse, Montana
Newly appointed sheriff Nick Rogers is hiding out in Montana from his murderous ex-partner. Despite adopting the local lifestyle, he's completely out of his realm, especially when being smitten with Laney Cavanaugh might blow his cover.

#1003 MIDNIGHT PRINCE by Dani Sinclair
When international playboy turned secret agent Reece Maddox teams with his mentor's daughter, will his secret identity be the only thing to unravel?

#1004 SPIRIT OF A HUNTER by Sylvie Kurtz
The Seekers
Dark and brooding Seeker Sabriel Mercer prefers to stick to the shadows. But when Nora Camden asks him to find her kidnapped son, the two will search the unforgiving White Mountains and find courage and love where least expected.

www.eHarlequin.com

HICNM0607